For Grant & Susan

Thank you,

Love, Jeff

Sunset Falls

Jeff Rosenplot

AuthorHouse™
1663 Liberty Drive, Suite 200
Bloomington, IN 47403
www.authorhouse.com
Phone: 1-800-839-8640

© 2009 Jeff Rosenplot. All rights reserved.

No part of this book may be reproduced, stored in a retrieval system, or transmitted by any means without the written permission of the author.

First published by AuthorHouse   1/9/2009

ISBN: 978-1-4389-3598-0 (sc)
ISBN: 978-1-4389-3681-9 (hc)

Printed in the United States of America
Bloomington, Indiana

This book is printed on acid-free paper.

For Sam. As is everything.

Contents

The Red Witch	ix
Sunset Falls	1
The Rules	21
Chores	31
A Walk In The Woods	39
The Goners	47
Overheard	55
Spirits	65
Augustus Dolarhyde	75
The Witch's Cabin	85
Huckleberry Browntree	95
Dutch and Penny	105
Last Goner Standing	115
Leap of Faith	127
Partial Credit	143
Sounds & Visions	153
Fear Itself	163
Talks by the Fire	173
Abigail's Note	183
Sacrifice	193
Dutch Comes Clean	207
The Truth, Plain & Ugly	223
The Miners Have Their Say	231
Fear	245
The Door	259
The Wild Card	271

SUNSET FALLS, WEST VIRGINIA, 1932

PROLOGUE

THE RED WITCH

They called her the Red Witch because they knew no other name for her. She wasn't a witch—far from it. But she was powerful and dangerous, and a witch was the closest anyone could come. The Red Witch was short, not even five feet tall, and nearly as wide around. She was American Indian, Sioux maybe or Lakota. Her skin was as brown as river mud. Her eyes were black like the mineshafts that interlaced the surrounding hills. She was not fearsome, and yet they feared her.

Sunset Falls, West Virginia was tucked deep inside the Appalachian mountain chain. It lay in a valley bordered on all sides by mountains and cloaked in a thick, ancient forest. The Red Witch lived in a cabin in the center of these woods. She never came into town. There were rumors about her. Sunset Falls was small enough, and insulated enough from the outside world, so that rumors and innuendo still had the power to become fact. In other places the Red

Witch and her dark powers would have been called myths. In Sunset Falls, they were part of everyday life.

She had appeared suddenly, no one remembered exactly when, and settled in as if she'd always been there. It was after the mines closed, after the Depression began. But it felt to everyone, even the oldest among them, as if she'd always been. She was part of the collective consciousness, the town's secret language. The town went on around her.

But to understand Sunset Falls, and to understand all that came later, it's important to know what lies at its core.

Coal mines were the lifeblood of not only this town, but also the entire state of West Virginia. It was dangerous, dirty, hard work, mining for coal, but so much of the world needed the black ore to survive that it was the only way most rural folks could make their livelihoods. The work was arduous but the pay made up for it. It was an honest living. Sunset Falls was a coal town, built up around the nearby Archer mine and miles from anything else. The townsfolk were solitary by nature, and proud of their self-sufficiency. They didn't want or need the outside world. If they didn't already have it, they certainly didn't need it.

It was that isolation that drew the Red Witch. A predator stays away from the larger herd, and a predator was what she was.

When the mine closed, the town decayed, rotting from the inside out. There was no work and there was no money, yet no one had the heart to leave. Their love of Sunset Falls kept the townsfolk rooted to it. But no longer being able to earn a living hollowed everybody out. Their emptiness and sadness was what drew the Red Witch to them.

The scope of reality in a small place like Sunset Falls was very narrow. If something fell outside their realm of experience, it was something to be feared. Much that happened after the arrival of the Red Witch was met with terror. Things changed. Familiar places became horrifying and foreign. The forest breathed and moaned with ominous shadows. No one ventured out after dark. Strange shapes lurked outside darkened windows. Awful shrieks echoed through the woods. They called her the Red Witch because they had no other name for her, and because it was she they blamed for turning their town into a haunted place.

In over-bright kitchens around hot mugs of homebrewed shine, the people of the town huddled close to each other. They were afraid not only for their lives but for their minds. The fear was driving them crazy. Most of the men had served in the Great War, fighting on battlefields a world away. They knew what it was to be frightened for their lives. What was happening in Sunset Falls was different, though—no one saw their enemies. They only heard them scurrying around after dark, and in the shadows, and just out of sight.

One such kitchen in one such house contained the town's elders.

They were men entrusted not by title but by character to lead the town out of its darkness. They were the town fathers, those with the keenest understanding of and the highest standing in the community. Reverend Martin was there, of course, and Dick Maloney, from the general store. Dalton Freewald sat between them, his fingertips still caked with years-old coal dirt. And Dutch Crosley, the farmer among them, and one of the only men who could make anything grow in the clay of the valley. They spoke in hushed tones, not wanting to be overheard.

"We don't even know who she is," Dalton Freewald said.

"It don't matter," Dick Maloney replied. "We wasn't afraid t'go out at night 'fore she came."

"An' that means it's all her doin'?" Dalton asked.

"Ain't the place for men to make God's rulin'," Reverend Martin said, and shook his head. "We don't know what manner of evil has come to our town. Maybe it's this woman, maybe it ain't. Maybe you put enough men outta' work long enough an' bad things just start happenin' on their own."

"An' maybe you outta' stick t'preachin' an' stay outta' workin' man's work," Dalton snapped.

"Way I see it," Dutch Crosley spoke up, "is that someone's gotta' go talk to her. If she ain't the cause of things, well, that's prob'ly for the best. But if she is, an' all the rumors about her is true, then maybe we can reason with her."

Dick Maloney snorted in disgust, but Reverend Martin nodded.

"It's the wisest course," he said in his most Sunday morning of voices. "And the hardest course. That's what makes it right."

"So who'll go?" Dalton Freewald asked. There was silence and the shuffling of cups.

"I'll do it," Dutch Crosley said. "My idea, seems only right I should go. 'Sides, wouldn't want none of you all t'wet your pants."

Dutch waited until the next day, of course. No one ventured out after dark, no matter what manner of diplomatic mission they were on. The other men walked with him to the edge of the Red Witch's clearing, and then Dutch went on alone.

The Red Witch's cabin was small and unremarkable. The paint on the wood siding was peeling. The roof needed shingles. It reminded Dutch of his own house, albeit only one story instead of two, and also… was the cabin moving? He stopped halfway up the path, stared hard at the porch. Yes, there, again, it was almost like it took a breath in, out, like a big heaving sigh. Dutch's blood ran cold. He'd been skeptical about all the Red Witch nonsense, never went in for that ghost and goblin baloney, but now, alone in the clearing, with the witch's house ahead of him, he wasn't so sure.

He took another step, carefully watching the house. It didn't move this time. He took another, watched the house again. Nothing.

A few steps later he'd convinced himself he was far too gullible.

The porch steps creaked with his weight. It was a nice, normal sound. He shook his head and knocked on the door.

It opened slowly and on its own. A small shadowy room with a large fireplace was the first thing he saw. The next was the Red Witch. She stood in front of the fireplace, nearly as wide as she was short. For a moment, he wanted to laugh. Then he didn't want to laugh anymore.

"Dutch Crosley," the witch said. Her voice was deep and brittle, an old person's voice.

"Ma'am, I've come on a behalf of the town," Dutch said.

"I know why you're here," the Red Witch replied. "Step inside, if you want to bargain."

Dutch stepped into the room. The door closed behind him.

"Sit down," the witch ordered. "Here, close to the fire."

As Dutch watched, the empty fireplace blazed to life, and a fire filled the room with heat and light. He sat down hard in a wooden chair.

"Dangerous happenings are afoot," the witch said. "Your town is at a crossroads. You need to make a choice."

"What kind of choice?"

The Red Witch smiled. There was nothing happy in the expression.

"What are you willing to sacrifice to make things right again?"

"You *are* the devil, then," Dutch whispered.

The witch shrugged. "Close."

"If we make a sacrifice, will things go back to normal?"

"If I am satisfied," she said.

Dutch nodded, slowly and deliberately. "All right, what is it y'want? You tell me an' I'll talk it over with the others and then –"

"What is your heart's desire?" the Red Witch asked. Dutch cocked his head, as if not understanding the question. In truth, he'd just never heard it put that way before. He knew his heart's desire. He would never tell.

The Red Witch smiled again, a reptilian look that made Dutch want to run.

"Y'cain't have that," he said.

Something was happening to the cabin. For a moment Dutch felt like he was shrinking, then he realized it was the walls. They were moving away from him. They got farther and farther away until at last he was surrounded only by darkness. He could see the witch, though, and himself, illuminated by the fireplace that seemed to hang in the middle of nothing.

"You love her," the witch said.

"I don't know whatcher –"

"You love your brother's wife, Dutch Crosley, and you can't have her and that only makes your desire burn stronger."

"No."

"Molly has no thought of you, does she? A farmer, an old man really with rough hands and a cruel heart. Not like your brother. He's a strong man, a young man, and he makes her happy."

"No!"

"You hate him for winning her heart and you hate him for leaving this town. You want to hurt him. *Bury* him."

"Stop it, please…"

"Show her to me," the Red Witch whispered. "Show me your heart's desire and your brother will suffer. Give me your heart's desire and I will be satisfied. Give her to me and you will be free."

Dutch closed his eyes. Molly's face bubbled to the surface. Her green eyes danced in his memory. Her red hair caught the sunlight from some long-ago day. She was his heart's desire, and his heart broke at the thought of her.

"Say her name and she is mine," the witch's voice echoed in his skull.

"I won't!"

"Say it!"

"I can't, please…"

"Say her name!"

"Forgive me."

"Say it now!"

"Molly..."

There had been good times. Once upon a time, and for a long time. Galen worked high up on the big buildings that rose like mountains out of Third Avenue. He was fearless as he walked the steel beams so high above the ground. There was always enough money. Galen was too tired, good tired, to talk about moving back home. West Virginia seemed a generation away, and his family...

Molly Crosley knew how to keep a secret. Crosley was her married name. Walker was what she'd known longer. Molly Walker was not of his people, small-minded, afraid. She had seen too much of the world to fear it. And Galen trusted her enough to leave them behind. It wasn't just love that they felt for each other, it was something even more. Like two halves of something long broken, finally and inevitably coming together. Galen and Molly couldn't have been more different, yet when they met the world stopped and they knew. Molly knew the consequences of loving a man like Galen Crosley. Misery would follow them, and it did, in time. But not before Abigail and then Benjamin were born, and the family knew happiness.

The Depression was where it began, but Molly knew more would follow. The dark troubles of the city and the lack of work paled next to the shadow that hung over them all. Galen didn't sense it, and the children, well, despite Abigail's strange perceptiveness and young Benjamin's fear of everything, they, too were consumed with the family's survival.

The shadow followed Molly for a long time. Like a bad dream, except it was a dream from which she couldn't waken. A blackness opened up inside her and began to swallow her deeper and deeper.

Galen found her lying half in and half out of their bed. It looked as if she was trying to escape what haunted her. In the end, though, she couldn't do it.

The Red Witch stayed where she was. She was hungry, and the town was afraid. Fear gripped the hearts of everyone, and fear was the most potent of emotions. The witch's shadow fell long across Sunset Falls, and its darkest days had just begun.

SUNSET FALLS 1934

Chapter One

Sunset Falls

Benjamin woke with a start. He looked around the bus. His blue eyes bit into Abigail like teeth, and for a moment she felt sympathy for her brother. Then it passed.

"Where are we now?" Benjamin asked.

"Not Manhattan," she sneered.

"I guessed that."

"I don't know where we are," Abigail shook her head. "Somewhere between where we started and where we're going."

"I dreamed again."

"About Mom?"

Benjamin nodded. "Bad this time."

Abigail Crosley was sixteen, tall, lanky and far too skinny. It had been a long time since she'd eaten properly. Dinner of late consisted of whatever she and her brother, Benjamin could scavenge. And that wasn't much. The bread lines were for the out-of-work men who hung about the streets and storefronts like sour-faced doorstops. The restaurants, (the ones that were still open, anyway), didn't throw very much food away. And the garbage cans were always guarded by gangs of boys, scrawny, rough-looking hoodlums who sneered and called out dirty things as she walked by.

They called it a "Depression," which was exactly how Abigail felt. From the moment her mother died, the world had gone out of focus. No one could tell them why she died. One doctor thought it was consumption, another thought it was tuberculosis. Abigail thought it might have just been sadness. No one knew for sure.

Everything spiraled away quickly after that. Their father stopped looking for work and the family lost their home. They stayed with neighbors for a while, but times were rough for everyone and there was only so much hospitality to go around. Abigail, Benjamin and their father bounced from one spare bedroom to another until there was nowhere else to go and nothing left to do but send the kids away.

The bus hit a pothole and shook Abigail's eyes open. She wasn't sleeping—she didn't sleep anymore. Hunger gnawed at her constantly. She didn't remember not being hungry. It invaded every thought she had, buzzing like a fly she couldn't squish.

She looked out the window. It was the same foggy green landscape she'd seen for the past dozen hours. Nothing but hills and dense green forest, and her own freckled reflection on top of it all.

She hated her freckles and her red hair. It announced her Irish blood like a sign around her neck. There was nothing interesting about her, nothing to set her apart in a city like New York.

She missed her city. Even watching it grind to a halt under the weight of the Depression, even seeing people living on the streets under cardboard boxes, Abigail loved New York. She wasn't born there, but she lived there. Really lived, too, because for her, walking out the front door was like setting out on a daily trip around the world. Wherever she went, she saw something incredible. On her way to school, past the fish market, past the Chinese firecracker factory, past the Jewish bagel shop, past the Italian restaurant where the old man, Jimmy Sparro, drank espresso coffee and called her "angel eyes"… it was the whole world in ten blocks, and it was *her* whole world. Now it was gone and here she was, sitting with her little brother on a bus bound for the deepest pit of nowhere.

"Will he be waiting for us?" Benjamin asked. He had a high-pitched, nasal voice that grated like rusty metal on Abby's nerves.

"Uncle Dutch knows we're coming," she said. "You read the letter."

"I'm scared."

"You're always scared."

"Not always."

Abby sighed, exasperated. "Look, Uncle Dutch and Aunt Penny

told Dad they'd take care of us. Do you think Dad would've sent us somewhere that wasn't safe?"

"No."

Abigail considered the question herself. She wasn't so sure about her own answer. After their mom died, their father had withered. He'd always been rowdy and playful and fun—Mom sometimes called him her third child. But after she died, and after everything else happened, he changed. He got darker. A shadow fell over him and he stopped being himself. Abby didn't recognize him sometimes. And sometimes she didn't want to.

"Have I ever met them?" Benny asked.

Abby shook her head. "Dad and Uncle Dutch had a fight a long time ago. Before you were born."

"About what?"

"Dunno. But I only met them once, and I was real little, two maybe, or just three. I can't remember much, just colors mostly."

"Why colors?"

"Because that's how memories work, idiot," she said. "I remember Dutch was big and gray, and that Penny was smaller and maybe blue."

"You're weird."

"And I'm not talking to you anymore."

The bus was nearly empty. A few people were scattered here and there, a soldier in uniform at the back, a young woman with a small child toward the front, and a short Native Indian woman. She was nearly as wide across as she was tall, and she kept glancing back at them. Something about the woman's dark eyes made Abigail shiver.

"What was their fight about?" Benny asked.

"I'm not talking to you."

"C'mon, what was their fight about?"

"Dad would never say," Abigail replied. "But they were brothers, they grew up together in Sunset Falls. It must've been something pretty awful for them not to talk for thirteen years."

"Do you think it was about me?" Benjamin asked. Abby laughed and shook her head.

"You really are an idiot, aren't you?"

Benny was about to reply when the bus driver turned around and shouted, "Comin' up on Sunset Falls."

Something fluttered in Abigail's belly, something different than her hunger. It was fear. She shook her head. Nothing to be afraid of. But she couldn't shake it. As the bus pulled off the highway, Abby felt a wave of nausea wash over her.

"You feelin' okay, child?" the Native woman asked. She was standing beside them now, and was so short that her eye level standing was the same as Abigail's sitting.

"I'm fine, yeah," Abby said. She didn't want to talk to this woman, something about her... another wave of nausea struck, and the woman put her hand on Abby's arm.

She felt like she was being burned. A pain shot through her body like an electric shock. Her ears started ringing and her heart raced. The woman smiled sweetly. Her round, brown face was smooth and unlined. She could have been any age, but Abigail felt she was very old. None of it fit. The woman's eyes were ice cold. Her warm smile didn't reach up into them. They were dark, too, darker and deeper than seemed natural. Abigail ripped her arm out of the woman's grasp.

"You be careful, child," the woman said. "This world's full of things you don't understand."

"Leave me alone," Abigail whispered.

The woman held her hands palms-up as she backed away down the aisle.

"Don't mean to hurt ya'," she said. "Just you mind the dark places. You got good reason to be afraid."

Abigail grabbed Benny's arm and pulled him down the aisle after her. She was terrified, and in a way no crazy New York street person could make her feel.

"Who was that?" Benny asked. "What did she mean?"

"I don't know, just, let's get off the bus."

They stumbled past the bus driver and down the steps. They had no luggage, and as they stepped off the bus the doors closed behind them. It pulled away in a cloud of blue exhaust.

"You're hurting my arm," Benjamin said, and Abby released her grip. She watched after the bus for a moment, but couldn't see the woman in the windows. Her heart slowed down and she started breathing normally again.

"What was that all about?" Benny asked.

"I guess there are crazy people everywhere," Abby replied. That answer seemed to satisfy Benny, but not Abigail.

They stood in front of a gas station. A handwritten "East Coast Bus Lines" sign was taped in the window. The gas station was directly off the two lane highway, and surrounded by dense green forest. There was no one around. The gas station itself looked deserted.

"What do we do now?" Benny asked.

"We wait," Abigail replied. "Uncle Dutch said he'd meet us. Maybe he's late."

"Maybe he's not coming."

"Shut up, Ben."

They sat on a bench in front of the gas station. It was cold, a damp cold that their flimsy coats didn't keep out. Benny's breath smelled stale. Abby heard his stomach rumble. As hard as everything was on her, she knew it was worse for her brother. He was thirteen but he was a young thirteen, certainly a lot younger than she'd been at his age. Where Abigail saw wonder, Benny saw only terror. Abby's restlessness made her curious. Benjamin just wanted to stay under the covers.

There was a rustling in the trees behind them. They turned to see a tall, thin man looking at them. He wore dirty coveralls and a ratty brown jacket, which was undone. His face was deeply lined. He had a thick grey beard that hung down to his chest. His eyes were hooded beneath bushy grey eyebrows.

"Uncle Dutch?" Abigail asked. Benny clung to her like he was drowning. She shooed him off.

The man stared at them for a moment. He stood at the edge of the forest, and looked like he might at any moment turn around to leave.

"You look just like your mama," he said. His voice was deep and rumbled in their ears. He spoke quietly, but his words carried with a power Abby didn't think could come out of someone so thin.

"I'm Abigail," she said, and stood up. Benny was close behind. They walked toward their uncle.

"This is Benjamin," Abby said, and extended her hand. Uncle Dutch glanced down at it as if he didn't know what to do. Then he nodded and shook it. His large, calloused hands had a tight grip.

"I s'pose I'm your Uncle Dutch," he said. Abby still couldn't see his eyes, shrouded as they were in shadow. She retrieved her hand and reached into her coat pocket. Abigail pulled out an envelope.

"This is from my dad," she said, handing the letter to Dutch. "He said he was sorry he had to trouble you. And he said he'd send for us soon."

Dutch nodded and took the letter. He put it in the pocket of his coveralls without looking at it.

"Your pa and me, we had some troubles," Dutch said. "But you all are kin, an' this is what kin does."

"You're a lot taller than Dad," Benjamin said. Abby slapped his arm.

"Your daddy was the runt," Dutch replied. "Now c'mon up to the house. Your Aunt Penny has a room set up for you, an' maybe you can have somethin' to eat. Y'all got some bags?"

Abby shook her head and Dutch shrugged. He turned around and led them into the forest. At first Benny was hesitant, but Abigail grabbed his arm and the two followed their uncle.

"Is your house in the woods?" Abigail asked.

"Other side of town," Dutch replied. "Not too far. Sunset Falls is a little place. Not like New York City, or wherever it is y'live. Sunset Falls keeps to itself. Not many strangers come through town."

"Is this a shortcut?" Abby asked.

Dutch shook his head. Sunlight fluttered in his hair, filtered by the trees.

"Ain't no road into Sunset Falls," he said. "Used t'be an old mining road, back when the mines was here. But the mines been closed for years now, an' the road's overgrown. Like I said, ain't many people comin' through town. We like it that way."

A short time later they stepped out of the woods and into Sunset Falls. It was a small town to be sure, a half dozen buildings gathered around a central square. A number of people were walking around, some going to the general store at the opposite end of the square and some going into a long, dark building with a sign above it that read, "SPIRITS". An old man sat on the steps of the small courthouse, eyeing them warily. Dutch waved to him and the old man nodded.

"You both wait here," Dutch said, pointing to a bench outside "SPIRITS".

"Where are you going?" Abigail asked.

"Got some business to do," Dutch replied. "Won't be too long. Don't go wanderin' off."

And then he was gone, slipping into the darkness of "SPIRITS". Ben and Abby sat down on the bench. It was warmer now—the sun was getting higher. The town was surrounded by hills, lush and green and taller than any of the buildings. It was almost like being in the bottom of a bowl.

"What kind of business do you think he's doing?" Benjamin asked.

Abigail snorted. "This is a bar, Ben. Uncle Dutch is going inside to drink alcohol."

Ben sucked in his breath. "But that's against the law."

"Not anymore," she replied.

Abigail took a long look around the square. The old man at the courthouse was still watching them. Abby ignored him. Instead she concentrated on a group of people standing in front of a building called "MILLER'S FEED & SEED". A man with a white collar was front and center, smiling broadly and gesturing grandly. Abby guessed he was a reverend, or maybe a priest. A small church stood across the street, behind the courthouse. He was addressing a group of people informally—no sermons today, just a friendly chat. There were two young women, a little older than Abby but not much. They wore plain brown dresses and simple black shoes, and their hair was pulled back into identical buns. A middle-aged man with a bushy black beard stood behind them. He fidgeted nervously with his hands. An older woman was also there, small and white-haired, holding a basket of bread. From time to time, they each glanced over at Ben and Abby.

"They're talking about us," Abigail said.

"Who is?" Ben asked.

"Don't look, geez, come on," she admonished. "Everybody's talking about us. I don't think they see too many new people."

"Dad really grew up here?"

Abby shrugged. "I can't believe it myself."

A man stepped out of the general store carrying a package wrapped in brown paper. He was thin and lanky, with round glasses that were so thick his eyes were magnified. His hair was long and in disarray and his coat was buttoned through the wrong holes.

Everything about him looked off-kilter.

"What did you say?" Abigail asked.

"I didn't say anything," Ben replied.

"Of course you did," she said. "Just now, I heard you say something."

"Not me."

Abigail shook her head. It was as if someone had whispered something into her ear, only not that close. It sounded like a whisper coming from a long way off.

"There, again, I just heard it," Abigail said. "You must be saying something. Knock it off."

"I'm not, I swear," Benjamin argued.

Abigail searched for the odd-looking man with the glasses, but he was gone. There was something different about him. He didn't fit in to the town. He hadn't stopped to talk with anyone, and he didn't even look over at the two strangers on the bench.

"I just heard you do it again," Abby said. "If you don't knock it off, Benny, I'm gonna' slug you."

"I'm not doing anything," her brother pleaded. "Seriously, Ab, I'm not. This place gives me the creeps. I just wanna' go home."

Abigail knew her brother well enough to know when he was lying, and this wasn't one of those times. So where was the voice she heard coming from? She looked around, trying to figure it out. It was like a whisper, or a group of whispers because more voices had joined the chorus. She stood up. The group of people around the reverend looked her way, but she didn't notice. Abby walked around the bench and headed for the back of "SPIRITS", thinking maybe someone was playing a trick on her. She got about halfway before a strong hand grabbed her shoulder. She spun around. Uncle Dutch glared down at her.

"Where you goin'?" he growled.

"I heard something," Abigail replied. "Voices. I wanted to see if - -"

"You heard voices?" Dutch asked. He looked nervous. His dark eyes got darker and his grip loosened on Abby's shoulder.

"I thought I heard whispering, and I wanted to see what was going on."

Dutch put his wide hand on Abby's shoulder and turned her around. "Ain't nothin' back there but forest. Best stay with your brother on the bench."

"But what is it?" Abigail asked. "What is that sound? You hear it too, don't you?"

Dutch shook his head. "I don't hear nothin'."

"Then why do you - -?"

"Some things in Sunset Falls is better left alone," Dutch replied. "C'mon, time to go home."

Abigail glanced over her shoulder into the dark woods. She got the feeling there was something more than what Uncle Dutch was telling her, but he seemed determined not to answer her questions. Ben shot her a pleading look that implored her not to leave his side. There would be time, she knew that. They weren't going anywhere.

The whispering voices got louder and denser as Abby and Ben followed Dutch through town. He nodded at the people they passed, and the townspeople regarded the new faces with a mix of wonder and disdain. Abigail knew they weren't welcome.

A path led from town toward the distant green hills. It was shaded by birch trees that stood like tall white soldiers in formation. Their branches entwined overhead, creating a canopy of leaves that turned the path into a tunnel. Dutch walked straight into the tunnel, but Abby and Ben both hung back.

"What's wrong now?" Dutch asked.

"I'm scared," Ben replied.

"Scared of what?"

"I don't know," Ben said. "It's just… I got a bad feeling."

Abigail had her own bad feeling, but not for the same reason. The voices had suddenly become very loud, almost loud enough for her to hear what they were saying. She knew that whatever was making the sound got stronger down the path. She also knew she didn't want to find out what it was.

"I've lived here my whole life," Dutch said. "And so did your Paw. Ain't nothin' down this path but houses an' forest."

"Come on, Ben," Abigail said. "Let's go. It'll be okay."

But even as she said it, she knew it wasn't true. Something was about to happen, or was already happening. And whatever it was, she had very little control over it. Events were moving faster than Abigail could keep track of. Ever since the Indian woman had grabbed her arm on the bus, and even before that, back when her mother died, she felt like something else was in control of her life. Abby felt like a passenger on an out of control carnival ride.

"Did you read my dad's note?" Abigail asked. Dutch shook his head.

"Don't need to," he said.

"But he told me to make sure - -"

"I know what he's gonna' say, so there ain't much point readin' it for myself."

Their uncle stopped. He sighed, and didn't turn around.

"Your dad and me, we just see things different," Dutch said. "But I know how much he loved your mom, and how much he loves you kids. And no matter what happened between us, he's still kin, and you're still kin."

"What did happen?" Ben asked.

Dutch looked over his shoulder. His eyes were hidden beneath his bushy gray eyebrows.

"That's between your dad and me," he said. "Ain't no reason t'talk about it now. What's past is past, and I think even your dad would agree with that. C'mon, your aunt Penny's waitin'."

They followed Dutch's stooped shoulders along the path. The forest was dark. Abby wasn't sure she'd ever seen a less hospitable place. Bushes and plants grew together like barbed wire, and the canopy of trees obscured nearly all the sunlight. It was a desolate place. Even though they were only a hundred yards from town, it felt like they were alone in the world. Ben's small hand grabbed Abigail's coat. She contemplated shaking him off, but she kind of liked the contact. She took his hand in her own and held on tight.

The forest path curved to the right, and then left again. They were surrounded—that was the feeling Abby got, as if the forest was flypaper, and the farther along they went the more stuck they got. They *were* out of control, Abigail knew that. And the forest wasn't the only thing trapping them. They were victims of their ages, children who trusted their parents to take care of them but when they couldn't, when the world conspired against them, Abby and her brother became castaways. And this place, this dark and foreboding woods, was their desert island.

The voices were louder now, not just whispers but distinct words.

"… didn't know you were…"

"… take me home now please or I will…"

"… lessons, more lessons…"

"… don't hurt me anymore, Mommy…"

"… understand why you won't…"

"Yes, soon."

Abigail clung to her brother. The trees themselves seemed to be speaking to her. Neither Dutch nor Benjamin reacted to the voices. She knew they didn't hear them. Maybe there was nothing to hear. Maybe it was only in her mind. But that thought was scarier than the voices. That meant there wasn't anything in the woods. That meant she was crazy.

"The house is this way," Dutch said. He stepped off the path and onto another, a smaller walkway that wound its way between the trees. Abigail smelled wood smoke. Somewhere a fireplace was lit. That meant someone else was out here, and that made Abby feel good for the first time all day.

They stepped into a clearing. A small wooden house was bathed in warm sunlight. Smoke rose from the chimney. The house was two stories, with a steeply sloped roof and two dark windows on the second floor. A porch wrapped around the front, and flowers were planted in boxes along the rail. Despite its weathered appearance, the house was inviting and, in comparison to the forest, almost cheerful. Beyond it, fields stretched into the distance. There was a barn, too, although it looked about ready to topple over.

An old woman stepped out of the front door of the house. She wore an apron and her white hair was tied up in a tight bun. Her face was pulled nearly as tight. Her lips were pursed and her eyes narrow. Her severity looked out of place among the warmth of the house in the clearing.

"These them?" she asked Dutch. Her voice had the grit of rough sandpaper.

"Abigail and Benjamin," Dutch replied, and then gestured toward the woman.

"This is your aunt Penny," he said.

Aunt Penny stared at them as if she'd found them on the bottom of her shoe. There was disdain in her cold eyes.

"You remind me of your mother," she told Abigail.

"Thank you," Abby replied.

"It weren't a compliment," Penny said. "And you, boy, you're the scrawniest thing I've seen since your father. Neither of you gonna' be much good to me."

"What is it you're expecting us to do?" Abigail replied.

"This ain't a free ride, girlie," Penny hissed. "This is a workin' farm. If you wanna' eat, you do your share. I'll be real honest with you… I don't want you here. Lord knows we got enough trouble feedin' our own mouths. So I ain't gonna' tolerate no sass talk or laziness. We live and die out here based on what we pull outta' the ground. If you don't think you can work hard an' keep your mouths shut, then turn around right now and catch the next bus outta' town."

Abigail fumed. The dislike she'd felt when first seeing Aunt Penny had blossomed into full-blown anger. She wanted to grab the woman's bun and twist it until her face warped into a kaleidoscope of eyes and nose and cheekbones. But she knew how desperate they were. She and Ben had nowhere else to go.

"Yes, Ma'am," she said.

"Yes, Ma'am what?" Penny asked.

Abigail seethed. "Yes, Ma'am, we'll work hard."

Aunt Penny regarded them for a long time. Then, satisfied that she'd gotten her point across, she turned around led Abby and Ben into their new home.

Chapter Two

The Rules

The house smelled like old people. Abigail remembered the smell from the Krycheks who lived down the hall. The Krycheks had worn their smell like a perfume, a combination of wet feet and sour armpits, but this house was different. The smell clung to individual molecules in the air until it was like walking face-first into a solid mass of odor. The smell was the same, feet and armpits, but it was more desperate, like the whole concoction was trapped in a damp dungeon with no prospect of escape. Abigail only wrinkled her nose—Benjamin clasped a hand over his face.

"Somethin' wrong?" Penny asked.

Benjamin started to respond, but Abby put a hand on his shoulder. She shook her head.

"Listen careful 'cause I ain't gonna' tell you twice," Penny said. "This is how things is gonna' work. You wake up at five a.m. every mornin'. Weekends, too. First thing you do, girlie, is go out to the well an' fill up the buckets."

"Abigail."

"What?"

"Abigail," Abby said. "My name's Abigail."

Penny looked cross. "Abigail, then. And you, boy, you're Benjamin?"

Ben nodded.

"Then, Benjamin, while your sister's fetching the water, you'll go out to the barn an' help your Uncle Dutch milk the cows an' collect some eggs. You, Abigail, you can cook, cain'tcha?"

"I can cook some," Abby said.

Penny snorted. "Bet you can. Scrawny thing like you. Too bad your Mama weren't around t'show you how to do it proper."

Abigail felt her cheeks flush crimson at the mention of her mother. She didn't want to hear Aunt Penny mention her mother. She didn't want her name to pass through those droll, wrinkled lips.

"Where do we sleep?" Benjamin asked.

"Upstairs," Penny replied. "In the attic."

"Together?" Abigail exclaimed.

"Ain't room t'give y'each your own quarters," Penny said. "'Sides, you'll appreciate the company. 'Specially after dark."

"What happens after dark?" Abigail asked.

Penny laughed and Abby's heart stopped. It was the coldest laugh she'd ever heard. Then Penny grinned a death's head grin and began reciting:

> *"When sunset falls in Sunset Falls,*
> *You'd best beware the banshee calls*
> *Your heart will seize from countless horrors*
> *If you find yourself trapped out of doors.*
> *With shapes that form from 'neath eerie light,*
> *Beware the things that go bump in the night.*
> *Make sure you're safe behind your walls,*
> *When sunset falls in Sunset Falls."*

Benjamin grabbed Abigail by the elbow, and threatened to rip her forearm off. Abby pried herself loose.

"What is that supposed to mean?" she asked. "We're a little old for ghost stories."

"Not old enough, I'm afraid," Penny replied. Her eyes narrowed. "Mind me close when I tell you this. Don't leave this house after sunset. And if you ever are outside when the sun goes down, find shelter. A house, a shop, someplace well lit. And never go into the woods. Stick to the paths. No matter what you see, or think you see."

Abigail's mouth was dry with fear. "And what will we see?"

Penny considered this, and nearly answered. But then she thought better of it.

"You mind me, is all," she said. "Sunset comes awful fast with these hills all around. Remember that. Don't never forget it."

"Not much chance of that," Benjamin replied.

Penny straightened her apron. "Since this is your first day, I'll let you get settled in 'fore I set you to your chores. Dinner'll be soon. Go upstairs an' I'll call you when it's ready."

Abigail took a deep breath. "Aunt Penny, I want to thank you for taking us in. I know it's not easy. We'll do what we're told."

Penny nodded and turned away, and disappeared into the kitchen.

Their attic room had one window that faced south, toward town. Abigail could see the tip of the church steeple over the trees. Two small beds were placed on either side of the window. An oil lamp sat on a table between them. Abigail lit the lamp.

"D'you think any of that was true?" Benjamin asked.

"Any of what?"

"That stuff she was saying, about not going out after dark."

Abby shook her head. "She's lying."

"What if she isn't?"

"She is."

"But what if she —"

"Stop it, Benny," Abigail said. "She's just having some fun with us. People in little towns don't have much. Although I don't think it was particularly funny."

"I can't sleep here," Ben said.

"You'd better learn to," Abby replied.

"Why couldn't we just stay with - -?"

Abigail wheeled around and nearly dropped the oil lamp.

"Look. There's something you need to understand and you've gotta' understand it quick. We're not going home. Dad dumped us here. He's not coming for us. Not today, not tomorrow, not ever. And if I have to share a room with you, you're gonna' need to understand that because there's no way I 'm going to listen to you whine about it. So get it into your head. This is all there is."

Benjamin was crying, but Abby didn't care. She was through with caring. Caring only hurt her—she cared about her mother, and look what happened. And Dad… he'd left them with these wretched people while he went off to do God only knew what. He'd failed them, that's what he'd done. He couldn't save Mom and he wouldn't save them.

"And quit whispering," she said. "It's driving me nuts."

"I'm not whispering." Ben sniffed back his tears.

"Fine, you're not whispering." She shook her head. "The moon'll be full in a couple of days. I won't have to listen to you anymore."

"What are you talking about?"

"Leaving," she said. "The jokers who live in this town won't go out after dark? Fine. It'll give me a good head start."

"You're running away?"

"I'm going home."

"But I'm afraid of the dark," Ben said. "How can I come with you if I'm - -?"

Abby lowered her head. The fire of her red hair caught the last of the valley's fading light.

"You're not coming. You're too young. I can't look after you and me, too. They may not be perfect, but Dutch and Penny will at least take care of you. They've promised that."

"I'm big enough to come."

"You won't even cut up your meat by yourself," Abby said, and sighed. "Besides, I don't want you to come with me."

Before Ben could answer, a loud ringing echoed across the valley outside. They both looked in the direction of the church steeple. A flock of birds took wing from nearby trees. The sound of the bells bounced across the hillsides and amplified.

"What's that sound?" Ben asked.

"Church bells, I think," Abby replied. "I wonder if there's a service tonight."

She pressed her nose against the window. It was nearly dark. The yard below was rutted with shadows. Abby saw Uncle Dutch running toward the house, and heard a door slam downstairs.

"Speak up, I can't hear you," Abby said.

"I already told you, I didn't say anything," Ben argued.

Abby shook her head, and whistled through her teeth. "They're really serious about this not going out after dark thing, aren't they?"

"What do you mean?"

"I think that bell is tolling sunset," she said. "The sun's going down over the hill. And Uncle Dutch just ran inside like he was being chased."

"You said it was all a lie."

"It is," Abby replied. "I mean, of course it is. It has to be. But these people don't seem to think so."

Ben put his hand on Abby's elbow. "What if it *is* real?"

She shook him off. "First of all, things like that don't happen. Second of all, even if it did, which it doesn't, there certainly wouldn't be any - - oh, God, what was that?"

Ben ran to the opposite side of the room, as far from the window as he could. He fell to the floor in a ball.

"I knew it was real, I knew it was," he cried. "It's worse than I thought and we'll never get out of here alive!"

"Shut up, Benny," Abigail said. "Something just flew past the window. Big, too. Kind of silvery."

"A demon, right? It was a demon?"

Abby looked disgustedly at her brother. "Are you kidding me? It was a bird or something. Maybe an owl. It sure was big, whatever it was. C'mon, Ben, get up and stop acting so feeble-minded."

"I'm not acting feeble-minded!"

Abby grinned. "So it's not an act, then? It's the real thing?"

"Shut up."

"Suppertime!" Aunt Penny called from downstairs. Her voice carried like a buzzard's shriek through the house.

"Come on, let's go downstairs," Abby said, and shrugged her shoulders. "Hey, at least there's one thing that's better here."

"What's that?"

"We'll definitely have something to eat."

"We haven't tasted it yet," Ben scoffed, and open headed out the door. He turned around when his sister didn't follow.

"You coming?" he asked.

"I've got to put the light out," she replied. Ben nodded and headed downstairs. Abby sighed. She hadn't meant to hurt him, at least that with such severity. Abigail didn't hate her brother. Sometimes she even kind of liked him. But she was sixteen, old enough to not have to put up with rules and chores from ancient relatives who were afraid of the dark. If being independent meant she had to leave Ben behind, well, it was good enough for their father, wasn't it? He trusted Dutch and Penny. Abby would have to do the same. And maybe someday she'd come back for her brother. She'd find a place to live, back home in the city, or maybe out west, California or even Texas. And she'd send Ben a bus ticket and he'd come live with her. Or maybe she'd never see him again. Settle someplace far away, maybe on a ranch or in the desert, and become one of those women who made pottery and Indian blankets and sell them by the side of the - -

"Abigail."

She spun around. The window was pitch dark now. Night had fallen fast over Sunset Falls. The oil lamp casts orange dapples across the glass. She stepped toward the window. Her heart beat hard. She knew the voice had come from outside the window, and yet… and yet every fiber of her body told her it hadn't, that it had been Aunt Penny calling her and it just *sounded* like it came from - -

She blew out of the flame. There was a face at the window. She only saw it for an instant, but it was a boy, handsome, her age, and silver-colored. Then it was gone before she could really see it, and she wasn't even sure if it had really been there.

"Whatcha' lookin' at?" Uncle Dutch asked. Abigail jumped. Concentrating on the window, she hadn't heard him come up the stairs.

"Nothing," she said. She even mustered a bit of a smile.

Dutch regarded her carefully. "You still hearin' voices?" he asked.

Abigail smiled. "Nope, not anymore. Must've been my imagination."

Dutch nodded, unconvinced. "Supper's ready. And your Aunt Penny don't wait for stragglers."

"I'm on my way," she said. Dutch's gaze lingered, and then he turned around and thumped back down the stairs.

Abigail turned back to the window. Whatever had been there was gone, if anything had even been there. She sighed and shook her head.

"Crazy must be contagious," she mumbled, and headed downstairs.

Chapter Three

Chores

They were up with the sun. Abigail, still half asleep, cooked the eggs her brother retrieved from the henhouse. Penny stood beside her.

"One-handed, you gotta' do it one-handed," she admonished.

"I can't do it one-handed," Abigail replied.

"Like this, watch me." Penny took one of the eggs in her large, red hand and tapped it on the side of the bowl. Mucousy liquid and a gelatinous yolk dribbled out. Penny threw the empty shell into a pail with other scraps.

"See?" she said. "Easiest thing there is."

The next two eggs that Abby tried to crack one-handed ended up raining shells into the bowl. Penny tsk-tsked and handed Abby a towel.

"Your hands are too small, just like your mother's," Penny said. "Those ain't farm hands. Too small an' too soft."

Abigail cracked the rest of the eggs two-handed while Aunt Penny fried some thick bacon on the stove beside her. It would've seemed almost sisterly, these two women side by side in the kitchen, had the tension not been so palpable.

Abigail cleared her throat. "I want to thank you again for taking us in."

Penny stiffened. "Weren't my decision."

"But we're here now, and I don't think much happens in this house without your say-so."

"Presume t'know how things run around here, do ya'?" Penny asked.

"I mean, I just - -"

"My husband is the head of this house," she said hotly. "You mind him as you mind me. Ain't his fault his brother up'n left his kids. Ain't mine, neither. But Dutch said we're takin' you in, an' that means we're takin' you in."

Abigail stirred the eggs. She was fixing them scrambled, all she knew.

"You don't like us very much, do you?" she asked. "Any of my family. My dad, my mom, me, Benjamin."

"Can't say as I do," Penny replied.

"Is it because we left Sunset Falls?"

"Why should I care an itch if you left Sunset Falls?"

"I don't know."

Penny flipped the bacon.

"You're comin' into this little town from on-high in New York City or wherever it is you're from, and you're thinkin', poor little country folk, ain't they quaint , ain't they so rural an' rustic," Penny said. "Sunset Falls ain't New York City, an' that's fine with me. I like knowin' the names of my neighbors. I like lookin' out my front window and seein' the same thing I always seen. If that makes me simple, then I'm proud to be so. But Sunset Falls ain't all quiet country livin'. We got bugs living under our skins an' they're fat with secrets. Dark secrets, the lot of 'em. So before you go makin' judgements about us here, or about why your parents left, think about this—we're able t'take you an' your brother in, feed ya', clothe ya' for Lord knows how long. We keep to ourselves, yes, but we take care of our own."

Penny drained the fat from the bacon and set it on a plate. She dropped more slices on the hot skillet. The meat sizzled.

"You had best remember your place here, little girl," Penny said.

"And what is my place?" Abigail fumed.

"You're an intruder," Aunt Penny hissed. "You're an uninvited guest. And I wouldn't be a bit surprised if all this trouble is somehow got to do with you."

"What are you talking about, trouble?" Abby asked.

"Penny, that's enough!" Dutch lumbered into the kitchen. He carried an armload of firewood. Ben followed close behind him.

"Breakfast ain't ready yet, Dutch," Penny said.

"Ain't breakfast that worries me," Dutch replied. He set the wood down beside the back door.

"You an' the boy wash up now," Penny said. "Abigail an' me, we're just workin' out an understandin'."

Aunt Penny glared at Abby. There was a smile on her lips, but her eyes were as cold as a February morning. A chill went up Abigail's spine. She wondered for the hundredth time since leaving the city if their father had even known what he was sending them into.

Their first "earnin' chore", as Aunt Penny called it, was scraping the old paint off the stables, and painting it fresh. They were given coveralls to wear, both pairs too large and awkward to effectively strip old paint. By noon, pieces of old paint clung to their sweat-soaked arms and foreheads.

"This is against the law," Ben said.

"It's not against the law," Abigail replied.

"It should be."

"Quit complaining. At least you only have to do the bottom."

"It's 'cause I'm shorter than you."

"Not by *that* much."

Abigail felt like she'd worked for three days instead of just a few hours. Her arms felt heavy and her whole body felt weak. She sighed.

"Ben, I can't hear you if you keep mumbling," she said.

"I didn't say anything."

"That was annoying when you did it yesterday," she told him. "Today it's just… ridiculous."

"I'm not - -"

"There, again, you just did it again."

"How can I be mumbling if I'm already talking to you?"

"I'm sure you've got it figured out."

"You're so weird."

"Y cain't be workin' if you're talkin'," Dutch called from inside the stable. A cow mooed.

"Quit mumbling," Abby hissed.

"I'm not!"

"It's not funny."

The whispers had gotten louder. She blamed Benjamin, but that was only for show. She knew it wasn't him. That was the only thing she *did* know. But if it wasn't him, well… if it wasn't Ben, it meant one of two things. One, she was crazy. Two, she really was hearing things. And neither option impressed her.

Something moved. She caught it in her peripheral, and spun around. She'd seen it between the stable and the woods. It was dark, and it moved fast.

"Did you see that?" she asked.

Ben dropped his scraper. "Oh no, what?"

"I saw it out of the corner of my eye, it went from over there and into the woods."

"What is it?" Ben whimpered.

"Relax, Hercules, it's probably just a - -"

She saw it again, this time to her left. She saw silver this time, and the billow of hair.

"It's all around us!" Ben wailed.

"We don't even know what it is," Abby cautioned. "Or even *if* it was any- -"

"I saw it, I saw it!" Ben cried. "It was a streak, it shot out past the stable. What is it?"

"I don't know. Did you get a good look at it?"

Ben shook his head.

"Me, neither," Abby replied. Her mind flashed back to the face she'd seen in the bedroom window. Had it even been a face? She knew what she'd seen. It was just a split second, but it was a face. She knew it was. And now this, a shadowy who-knew-what neither she nor Ben could get a good look at.

Dutch appeared suddenly, looking flushed and excited.

"In the house," he said.

"But our chores aren't done," Ben whined.

"Chores'll wait," Dutch replied. He nervously scanned the woods.

"What's out there?" Abigail asked.

"Don't know whatcha' mean."

"Of course you do."

"Reckon I don't," he said. "And I'd quit worryin' my own head about it if I was you."

"But we both saw something."

"Did ya'?" Dutch asked. "Then tell me what you saw. Cain't do it, can you? That's 'cause there ain't nothin' there."

"There is and you know it!" Abby was indignant.

"An' you need t'remember who's in charge here," Dutch said. "Some stones in Sunset Falls is best left unturned. You wanna' get along here? You wanna' know the secret? Come in the house when I tell you to, and don't look back. That's the best advice I can give ya'."

Reluctantly, Abigail followed her brother and uncle across the dead grass to the house. The whispers became louder, and she was certain something was watching them.

Chapter Four
A Walk In The Woods

The moon was full.

It took Benjamin a moment to recognize that when he woke. The light from the moon was so bright that he was nearly convinced it was morning. Then the realization hit him, and he was afraid.

Abigail was gone. He knew she would be—she always did what she promised. She'd left a note, as well. Ben knew it without even finding it. He could even recite it, sight-unseen: "Dear Benny, I can't stay here anymore, blah, blah, blah, not your fault, blah, blah, blah, Dutch and Penny will be good to you." Abby believed in her own judgment. She was never wrong. And yet here he was, alone with relatives he was afraid of, and where was she?

That was a good question. Where *was* she? She couldn't have gotten far. The moon had only just risen over the mountaintops. That meant it wasn't much past midnight.

A breeze blew the wind chimes that hung on the porch. Even

through the closed bedroom window he could hear them. Their lonely wooden jingle called out to him. Now or never.

Benjamin got dressed quickly. He kept his shoes off as he tiptoed down the stairs. He heard Uncle Dutch snoring. Aunt Penny wheezed in her sleep beside him.

The night air was cool but refreshing. If it had been darker, he would have been more afraid. As it was, though, it was as bright as morning under the moonlight.

"She'll head for the road," he said. He thought his own voice might spook him, but instead he found it reassuring. He tied his shoes and headed into the woods, in the direction he supposed his sister would go.

Ben Crosley was a young thirteen. He was his family's baby, his mother's baby especially. He knew Abby resented that, so he was helpless for her sake. It gave her something to despise, and since she'd reached puberty she'd begun to despise everything. Ben was different than that. He aw-shucks'd his way into being a teenager, almost backed into it. Where Abby was all about mood swings and sullen fury, Ben was almost lazy about it. He was a smart boy—smarter than most people knew, including Abby. But he was content to let the world happen. His sister was in charge of the brimstone and the hellfire. Ben just wanted to make sure they followed the same path home.

Their mom's death had sucked Ben's heart out of his chest. And for a while, it had sucked the fire out of Abigail's belly. They were both haunted by the loss, and it was only together that they managed to survive it. And as the Depression got worse, Ben held on to their togetherness as the tenet of his improvised faith. Only together could they make it through. And now Abby was gone. Benjamin meant to get her back. If she couldn't see how important it was for them to stay together, then he'd realize it strong enough for the both of them.

The moonlight wasn't as bright in the woods. The dense trees kept most of it out. Pools of silver light cut through the branches and made strange shadows on the ground around him. A soft breeze rustled the leaves. Walking through the woods didn't seem like such a good idea anymore. Ben's hands were clammy, and his heart started beating faster. Ben was afraid, and wondered why Abby would ever think of leaving him alone.

Abigail knew she wasn't alone. It wasn't just the shadows of the forest that spooked her. She was being followed.

There was no path to stick to. From the clearing around the house, she'd seen the spire of the church and pointed herself in that direction. But the woods had turned her around. She knew she should have reached Sunset Falls long ago. The moonlight disoriented her. Its shimmer led her astray, making her see a clearing where none existed, and shapes she couldn't reconcile. She was beyond lost now. All she could hope was to stumble blindly onto a way out.

There was definitely something following her. It had been behind her but now it was pacing her, off to the right. A bear? Maybe. Or a cougar.

or whatever it is that haunts this town

No, that was stupid. All that talk, that ridiculous poem

when sunset falls in Sunset Falls

it was all some elaborate hoax, maybe a way to keep strangers off balance. Something was in the woods with her, and it was more real and solid than some boogeyman. Abby walked faster. A twig snapped to her right. Closer this time. Nearly on top of her.

Panic took hold. She ran. She didn't know where she was running, only that it was away from whatever

whoever

was following her. The forest blew past her in a shadowy blue streak. She tripped, but righted herself. Her heart beat furiously. It was keeping pace with her. It was nearly on top of her. She ran faster. It hurt to run. Her muscles stung and her lungs burned.

She collided and screamed at the same time. She landed on her back in a pile of leaves. The moonlit clearing blinded her. She couldn't see what she'd hit. She got to her feet and whirled around.

"Ben?" she asked. Her brother lay on the ground. She'd run into him hard, and he groaned his reply.

"What are you *doing?*" she asked.

"Looking for you," he said, and immediately his eyes grew huge. "We've got to go. Something's following me."

"That was me, dopey," Abby said, then shook her head. "Don't feel too bad, I thought you were something following me."

Benjamin sighed and got to his feet.

"I thought I was quiet enough that you wouldn't hear me leave," Abby said.

"You were. It was the moonlight. The moon's full. I remembered what you said."

"You got my note, then?"

Ben shook his head. "I didn't read it."

"Why not?"

"I didn't have to. I know why you left."

"So what are you doing here, then?" she asked.

"You've made a mistake, is all."

"Have I?"

"Yeah, and I'm gonna' make sure you don't completely mess things up for yourself."

Abby glowered. "And how do you think you're gonna' do that?"

"By bringing you back to Uncle Dutch and Aunt Penny," Ben

said. He shook his head. "Look, Dad's not gonna' leave us here forever."

"Don't count on it."

"He won't. He'll come and get us, and he'll come soon. We just gotta' stay here and wait for him. Otherwise how will he find us?"

Abby threw up her arms in exasperated fury.

"Ben, wake up! When Mom died, so did Dad. He gave up on us. *That's* why we're here, not some story that he can't find work and it's better for us to live with kin. He hasn't had regular work in three years but we've gotten by. What's different about this time? I'll tell you what… nothing. He's just done with us, Benny. We remind him too much of Mom. He cried himself to sleep, did you know that? I'll bet you didn't. No one should ever hear their Dad cry. It's an awful sound. Almost worse than anything. Because it means things are worse than you can imagine. If Dad can't handle it, how can we?"

They were quiet for a time. Abby kicked at the ground with the toe of her well-worn shoe. She'd said more than she intended.

"You could've taken me with you," Ben said. His voice was small.

"Yeah, maybe," she relented.

"We can go now," Ben said, excited. "We can find the road and go together. That'll be okay, won't it? Since I'm here and all?"

"No."

"Why not? That's not fair!"

Abby put a hand on Ben's arm. "Because there's something else out here."

Ben grabbed tight hold of his sister.

"Let go," Abby said.

"I can't."

"Let go, Benny."

"Why?"

"Because we've gotta' run!"

Abigail pulled Ben headlong across the clearing. They stopped dead halfway there.

It was a girl, or had been. Her face was contorted into a grimace, and large pieces of her hair and scalp were missing. She was bone white and, despite everything Abby's mind told her to the contrary, was also transparent.

"What *is* that?" Ben asked in a choked voice.

Before Abby could answer, the thing opened its mouth and emitted a scream that made their blood freeze. The sound was unlike anything either of them had heard before. Halfway between a hawk's cry and a baby's painful wail, it echoed through the forest. Abby and Ben screamed themselves. It was all they could do. But their own screams were rendered mute by the wailing of the

banshee

yes, banshee, that was all it could be, the shrieking creature of folklore, screaming from the Irish hillsides when death was near. Its shrieks made them fall to their knees and cover their ears. Abigail thought she'd never be able to hear again. All that went through her head was Aunt Penny's poem, "When sunset falls in Sunset Falls, you'd best beware the banshee's calls." Oh, God, she'd been telling the truth.

And then it stopped, and the woods were silent. For a moment, Abby kept her ears covered. Slowly she lowered her hands. She looked around the clearing.

There were five of them, including the banshee girl. They surrounded the clearing in pools of silvery transparent white light. There was another girl, angry, with broad shoulders and furious eyes; a black-skinned giant who could have been any age, shirtless and with a rope hanging from his neck; a well-dressed European man in a waistcoat and knickers, who reminded Abby of pictures she'd seen of Mozart; and the fifth, the boy whose face she had seen at her window, handsome and sweet, with kinder eyes than any of the others.

Beside her, Benjamin fainted. His small body slipped into the grass of the clearing. That broke Abby's paralysis, and she bent down to him.

"Child of the Walker," the angry girl bellowed. "It's time to face your fate."

Chapter Five

The Goners

Abigail glared at the wild-eyed girl. They were about the same age, and roughly the same height. That was where any similarity ended. The girl's silvery body could be seen clean through, so that the forest behind her was clearly visible. She wore a dress of some nondescript shape and material, which fluttered slightly even though what little wind there had been had died away. She appeared solid despite her transparency, all except for her legs, which ended not in feet but in a transparent mist.

"Come forward, Walker's child," the girl said.

"That's my mother's maiden name," Abby said. "How do you know my - -?"

"She doesn't know anything, Alice," the boy said, and Abby turned to face him. He was also silver and transparent, but his clothes were contemporary. Abby had seen similar outfits, dungaree pants and a white collared shirt, on many of the men at bus stops on the way to Sunset Falls.

The wild-eyed girl, Alice, spun around to confront the boy. Her eyes were furious, and her kinky, curly hair seemed electrified.

"Of course she knows," Alice spat. "It runs through her blood."

"She doesn't know," the boy said again. "She's an innocent."

"There are no innocents."

"Don't you think that maybe - -"

Alice moved so quickly that Abby barely registered it.

"Don't let your personal feelings get in my way," Alice hissed, face-to-face with the boy. "I wonder, sometimes, if it was such a good idea to let you in. You were lost before we found you. Don't forget that. You can get lost again."

The boy lowered his eyes. "I don't know that that would be such a bad thing."

Alice glared at him for a moment, then spun around to face Abigail.

"You are the child of a Walker," Alice said, "and yet I'm beginning to believe you are ignorant of your legacy. Is such a thing possible?"

"What *are* you?" Abby asked.

The banshee girl laughed, a sound almost as shrill as her screams.

"Baby Millie thinks you're a fool," Alice said. "I myself don't believe that."

"How do you know my mother's name?" Abby asked. "She hadn't

been Molly Walker for a long time."

"Hadn't been?" Alice smiled. It was a cruel expression.

"She's dead," Abby said bluntly.

"You seem quite certain of that."

Abigail's eyes narrowed. "What are you talking about? Who *are* you people?"

"Sie is unwissend!" the Mozart look-alike shouted. He had sat down in the clearing, except he was sitting six inches off the ground.

"Leopold also believes you are unaware of the facts," Alice said. She moved away from Abby, and this time Abby clearly saw her float.

"You're ghosts," she said in a hushed whisper.

"See, she's not such a fool," Alice said.

Abby shook her head. "But that's not - -"

"Possible? *Everything's* possible."

"Not this," Abby replied.

"It's too much for her, Alice," the boy said. "She can't handle it."

"No, this one's strong," Alice replied. "Strong of mind, strong of heart. A long time have I waited for her. Long before you, Augustus Dolarhyde, and your "accident". Your weak character brought you to us. I won't have it sabotage what I've waited generations to find."

"You're crazy," Augustus Dolarhyde said.

"You try waiting a hundred and eighty years to pass over, let's see how much patience you have." Alice's eyes flashed a cold blue, and

Augustus backed away.

"There are things you think you know," Alice said, turning once again to face Abigail. "About life, the world, the way of things. I'm here as," she laughed, "living proof that none of it is true. Pardon the irony."

"Bitten Sie sie, mir meine Schuhe zugeben!" Leopold shouted.

"She doesn't have your shoes!" Alice snapped. "No one does. That happened ninety years ago."

"We forget about time," Augustus said. He floated across the clearing and stood beside Abigail. He was close enough to touch, but she didn't dare.

"You're all dead?" Abigail asked.

Augustus Dolarhyde nodded. "I'm the newest. Alice is the oldest. The rest of them, Baby Millie, Leopold, Abraham, the silent giant over there, they were all together before I came."

"Before we found you," Alice said, and turned to Abby. "Poor little Gus is a tender soul. He makes a terrible Goner."

"Goner?" Abby asked.

"Alice's idea," Augustus sighed. "She overheard someone use the expression, 'he's a goner', and it just stuck."

"You're called 'The Goners'?"

Gus shrugged and Alice scowled.

"What happened to *you*?" Abby asked.

"She won't tell," Gus replied. "Alice likes to keep a shroud of mystery around herself."

"Enough!" Alice roared. "This is the Walker's child, there is no doubt, and regardless of what she knows, she is still fair game."

"Fair game?" Abby asked.

"We know another Walker has invaded our land," Alice told the other Goners. "It lives in these woods and feeds on the fear we have planted. That is *our* harvest. We have worked too hard to allow some Red Witch to stake a claim here."

"But she's too powerful," Gus said. "You've said so yourself. We're only spirit. The Red Witch is living form."

"So is this Walker's child," Alice replied.

"She won't do it," Gus said.

"Not willingly."

"I won't let you do anything to her."

Alice laughed harshly, like a sputter. "Your threats are hollow. Stand in the shadows as long as I have, boy, and watch everything you know rot away before your eyes. Watch the life that was stolen from you wither and die and everyone you ever cared about buried in the earth, and then you can play your valiant white knight. Until then, do as you're told."

Baby Millie shrieked with laughter. Alice floated across the clearing, leaving a trail of blue vapor.

"What is this 'Red Witch'?" Abigail asked. "You said she was a

Walker. Is she some sort of distant relative of mine?"

Alice shook her head. "A Walker isn't your family name, although your mother used it as such. Clever creature, because doing so allowed her to move freely among the living world. No, a Walker is a being that spends its days in pursuit of emotion. The more powerful the emotion, the more powerful the Walker becomes."

"It's a vampire, then?" Abby asked.

"No, it's a scavenger, it lives on the byproducts of human emotion. Every feeling, every joy, every sorrow sends a ripple into the ether. A Walker can sense these ripples like a vulture and uses the energy to grow strong."

"What does my mother have to do with any of that?" Abigail asked.

Alice laughed again, and shook her head. "Maybe you are a fool, after all."

"My mother… was a Walker?" Abby was dumbfounded.

"*Is* a Walker," Alice replied. She stared hard at Abigail.

"Your mother can't die," Alice said. "Just as we can't die, neither can she. Neither can any Walker."

"But you're ghosts," Abby replied. "You're already dead."

"If only that were true," Alice said.

"What are you, then?"

"In transition," Alice explained. "Permanently, or so it would seem. Not alive, no, but most certainly not dead."

"She doesn't understand," Gus sighed.

"Yes I do," Abby replied. "I don't believe it, but I do understand it."

"Then you must have some idea of what she wants to do with you," Gus said.

"Me? But I'm not a Walker."

"You are a half-breed," Alice said. "And that is the rarest of finds. To have blood in your veins from both worlds…"

"Ich wünsche meine Schuhe!" Leopold yelled.

"Enough with the shoes!" Alice bellowed. "When they killed you, they took your shoes. I've explained that to you."

"Leopold was only in America for a day and a half," Gus told Abby. "He was on a train from New York, heading out west. Two men killed him. All they took were his shoes."

"Gebe mir meine Schuhe!" Leopold whined.

"You don't even have feet anymore," Alice said. "Look at you! There's only vapor down there. What would you even *do* with shoes?"

"He can't understand you," Gus said. "I'm not even sure how you can understand him."

Alice shook her head and addressed Abby again.

"You are the product of two separate worlds," she said. "You are the only half-breed child your Walker mother produced."

"No, there's Ben, too," Alice replied, and instantly regretted it.

Gus shook his head. "Walkers are only female. Half-breeds, too."

"So my father - -?"

"Human," Gus replied. "Mortal. The other half of your half-breeding."

"Enough with the history," Alice roared. "Walker child, half-breed, your time is over. You belong to us now."

Before Abigail had time to react, a blinding white light blanketed the clearing. The Goners were nearly invisible within it. It had no source that Abigail could see, but it filled every nook and cranny and crag and hollow around them. Baby Millie shrieked, but even that awful sound was muffled. The light was like a snowfall, dulling all sounds, even Abby's ever-present whispers.

Abigail felt hands grip her shoulders, strong hands, and she was lifted up. Ben was beside her, unconscious but being carried along, as well. They were carried through the woods, and as the brilliant light grew dimmer, Abby's mind shut down and she knew no more.

Chapter Six

Overheard

Abby woke with a start. The sun was high and it brightened the attic room. She was in her bed, or at least the bed she slept in at Dutch and Penny's house. Ben was still asleep.

For a moment, she thought it was a dream. But she'd dreamed before, and this wasn't like that. It had really happened, no matter what she wanted to think.

She sat up in bed and let out a small shriek. Aunt Penny stood at the end of her bed. She didn't move, only glared down at Abby. There was hatred in her eyes.

"You were out last night," she said. Her tightly drawn lips were even more so now.

"I don't know what you're - -"

"Lying is a sin," Penny said. Beside them, Ben woke up but didn't say anything.

"What I do is my business," Abby replied calmly.

Penny's eyes narrowed. "Your insolence will not be tolerated in this house."

Abby got out of bed. She was still in her clothes from the previous night.

"I'm not taking orders anymore," she said. "Not from you or Dutch or anyone else. I don't know why you and this town are so afraid of everything, but I'm beginning to find out. And I'm beginning to find out that you need me a whole lot more than I need you."

"You're as crazy as your mother."

"You didn't know my mother!" Abby screamed. "And you don't know me. Now, I've tried to be nice to you, and I've tried to be polite, but that obviously doesn't work. So I'm going to be blunt. Don't come near me or my brother again. We're going to leave soon. For good. But not before I find out what's going on, and what happened to my mother."

"You *should* leave," Penny said. "I din't want you here, anyhow. But if you think you're gonna' find your answers here, you're makin' a big mistake. This town is as tight-closed as a bear trap. We didn't need your mother, an' we certainly don't need you."

Aunt Penny spun around and clopped in her thick shoes down the stairs. Abigail lowered her eyes and let out a long sigh.

"What was that all about?" Ben asked.

"Never mind."

"Tell me, Abby, c'mon. What's going on?"

Abby shrugged. "It sounds crazy to even talk about it. I mean, with the sun up and everything, it almost does feel like a dream."

"What does?"

"You don't remember?"

Ben squinched his eyes in concentration. "Well, the last thing I remember is going into the woods to find you, and then I *did* find you, and then… wait, there was someone else there, wasn't there?"

"Yeah, there was."

"Who was it?"

"You really don't remember?"

"Nope."

"That's right, you fainted."

Ben was indignant. "I did not faint!"

"Fine, passed out, then. Point is, you were out of it. But how did we get back here?"

"Back here? What do you mean?"

"I mean, I remember what happened after you passed out, but then I must've passed out, too, because I can't remember how we - -"

"I hear them," Ben said. His voice was a terrified whisper.

"You hear what?"

"Your voices."

Abby raised an eyebrow. "You do?"

"Mumbles, right?"

"Yeah."

"They're coming from the heating vent," Ben said, pointing to a metal grate low down on the wall. Abby walked around Ben's bed and knelt down beside the grate.

"You hear 'em?" Ben asked.

"Of course I do, it's Dutch and Penny downstairs," Abby snapped. "Now ssh, or they'll hear us."

Ben knelt down beside her, and together they pressed their ears to the grate.

"… still don't know what happened out there," Dutch said.

"Somethin' sure did," Penny replied.

"Maybe it was the Red Witch."

"Or maybe it was the angel Gabriel," Penny retorted. "I don't trust the lot of you, Dick Maloney, Dalton Freewald, even that Reverend Martin. I don't know what you've all got yourselves up to."

"We got the girl back, that's the point."

"That *ain't* the point," Penny said. "She knows what's goin' on now."

"No she - -"

"Not all of it, no but enough t'get her hackles up. She ain't gonna' be so easy to keep control of as we thought. You made us a bad deal, Dutch Crosley. Just hope this girl's able t'undo the mess you made."

"I ain't gonna' apologize t'you."

"No, I wouldn't expect you to. You're too selfish and stubborn for that. And it ain't about me, anyhow. Sure, I got things t'say t'you, any wife would, but that's my cross t'bear. This is a whole lot bigger'n you'n me."

Dutch shifted in his chair. "Dick Maloney thinks we oughtta' just cut our losses an' get it over with now."

"Any sentence that starts with 'Dick Maloney thinks' is doomed from the get-go," Penny said. "No, it ain't time yet. The girl's still too headstrong. Shoulda' heard how she talked t'me just now. No, we gotta' wait a little while more. Let her get closer to it all. She'll weaken up."

"And if she don't?"

"I ain't met one of them yet what can stand up to the kinda' things we got livin' in them woods."

"The Red Witch has."

"The Red Witch is gettin' weak herself," Penny said. "Them Goners ain't never been so brave before. Comin' right out like that."

"You think *they're* gonna' win out in this?" Dutch asked.

"Ain't nobody gonna' win out in this but this town," Penny said. "I ain't lived here all my life so's I can watch it get swallered up by some hole in the fabric."

Dutch pushed back his chair. "I'm leavin'."

"Where you goin'?"

"Into town. Maybe 'SPIRITS'."

"I hate your weakness, Dutch. You give in to your vices far too easy."

"My vices is all I got left."

The screen door slammed and Dutch left the house. Abby scrambled to her feet and watched him cut across the grass and disappear into the woods.

"What was *that* all about?" Ben asked.

"It's about what happened last night," Abby told him. "We're in the middle of something here that's really, really big. And I think maybe Mom's involved in it, somehow."

"Mom? How could she be - -?"

"They were ghosts, Benny, what we met in the woods. What made you faint, sorry, pass out. There were five of them. They called themselves the Goners."

"You said none of that was real," Ben said.

"I was wrong."

"You're never wrong."

"This time I'm wrong."

Ben shook his head. "It's not funny, Abby. Really. You know how scared I am about being here. And that poem Aunt Penny told us… I don't need any help scaring myself."

Abigail sighed, exasperated. "So why did you come looking for me if you were so scared?"

Ben kicked at the floor. "'Cause I was more mad than scared, I guess."

Abby nodded. "It means a lot that you came after me."

"It does?"

"And for what it's worth, I'm sorry I didn't take you along in the first place. I was wrong."

"Wow, twice in one day."

Abby grinned. "Don't push it."

Ben smiled broadly. "But we can go now, right? Together? It's daytime now, we can make it through the forest and find the road before it's dark. Ta-da! No more ghosts!"

Abby sat down on her bed. "They told me something about Mom," she said, " the ghosts did. Something I'm not sure I even really believe."

Ben sat down beside her. "What is it?"

"You know Mom's maiden name was Walker, right?"

"Right."

"Well, the Goners told me that wasn't exactly true."

"What did they say?"

"That she was a sort of ghost herself," Abigail replied. "She was something *called* a Walker, sorta' like a scavenger that lives off human emotion. And that she fell in love or something with Dad, and she lived like a regular person."

"That's crazy."

"That's what I thought, too, except the one Goner, Alice, the leader, she said that Mom couldn't die, that it was impossible for a Walker to die."

"But that would mean - -"

"Yeah, exactly," Abby nodded. "Mom might be alive."

Ben lowered his head and covered his face.

"You okay?" Abby asked.

Ben nodded, and wiped tears away.

"Do you believe them?" he asked.

Abigail shrugged. "I don't believe in ghosts, but I still had a conversation with some last night. Do I believe Mom's alive? I want to. And I'm trying to separate that wanting from the problem of figuring out what's really going on here."

"Dutch and Penny!" Ben exclaimed. "The conversation through the vent. They know, don't they?"

"They know something, that's for sure."

"So let's ask them," Ben said.

Abby shook her head. "They won't tell us anything. There's something else going on in Sunset Falls, and I think it has to do with us. Me, in particular."

"What about me?"

"The Goners told me that Walkers are only female," Abby said. "They called me a half-breed. There must be some meaning to that, more than what I can understand. It seemed like they wanted something from me, or something I had."

"Like what?"

Abby shrugged. "Dunno'. I think they were gonna' try to hurt me."

"Then we really do gotta' leave," Ben said.

"If what they said about Mom is true, and she really is still alive, then we've got to find her."

Ben threw up his hands. "For all you know, they could've been lying to you about that."

"But why?" Abby asked. "What would they gain by lying to me? They were fully intending to do something to me. For all I know, they might've even killed me. There was no reason for them to lie."

Ben shook his head. "What about that Red Witch Dutch and Penny talked about?"

"The Goners talked about that, too," Abby said. "She's a Walker, too, and a powerful one, by the sounds of it. Even the Goners were afraid of her."

"I wish we could ask someone," Ben said. "Aunt Penny would never answer our questions."

Abigail cocked an eyebrow. "Uncle Dutch might."

"But you said he and Penny - -"

"Not here, he'll never talk here, but maybe somewhere that Penny isn't," Abby said. "Somewhere like - -"

"'SPIRITS'!" Ben jumped up.

"We can catch him if we hurry."

Chapter Seven

Spirits

Abigail had never been inside a bar. It was largely due to her age, but also because, until very recently, drinking alcohol had been against the law. Stepping through the door of 'SPIRITS' was like stepping into forbidden territory.

The bar was dark and smelled stale. Each of the three windows was covered with dark shades, pulled tight. The only light came from dim lamps on the small tables, and a half dozen bare bulbs behind the long wooden bar. Three men sat at the bar, two in front on stools and the bartender behind it. They glanced at her scornfully as she walked in, and then returned to their conversation. It took a moment after the door closed for her eyes to adjust to the dark. Once they did, she spied Uncle Dutch in the farthest corner. He was alone at a small table. She walked over to him and sat down. He glanced at her, but didn't seem surprised.

"Your aunt know you're here?" he asked.

"What do you think?"

Dutch snorted and took a drink from the glass in front of him.

"You ain't s'posed t'be in here," he said.

"Neither are you."

"Prohibition?" he asked. "That nonsense don't matter much out here. 'Sides, I heard it was all over with. The taps is flowin' again!"

Dutch raised his voice for the last part, and the men at the bar, a skinny man with sunken eyes and another, rounder man with only a halo of brown hair on the sides of his head, laughed.

"Sorry I cain't offer you a drink," Dutch said.

"That's not why I'm here."

"I know why you're here."

"My mother."

Dutch ran a thick hand through his hair.

"You ain't gonna' start with an easy one, is ya'?"

Abby shook her head. "All the other questions I have come back to her, so why not start at the source?"

"Them things in the woods…"

"The Goners."

Dutch snorted. "The Goners, yeah. They the ones that told you about your Ma?"

Abby nodded.

"Thought so. What did they say?"

"You want to make sure you get your story straight?"

"I ain't tryin' to - -" he said loudly, but when the other men in the bar looked over, he lowered his voice.

"Let me make one thing real clear," Dutch said quietly. "When your Ma came to Sunset Falls, there weren't nobody was unaffected by her. She was the most beautiful thing any person in this town every seen. It was like she cast some sorta' magic spell over us. And in a way, that's just what she did. Them Goners told you she was a Walker?"

Abby nodded.

"Well, there's more than one kinda' Walker," Dutch said, and shook his head. "We all found that out the hard way."

"More than one kind?" Abby asked. "What do you mean?"

"Your Ma, she was, I dunno', she was a good kinda' Walker," Dutch said. "She lived off good things, good feelin's, positive energy. An' every bit of the good she took in seemed to come right back out. She made everyone feel good, no, more than good, even. It was part of her magic."

"So what happened?"

Dutch raised an eyebrow and cocked his head. "We all fell in love with her, the whole town, but it was your dad, my little brother Galen, who changed in all. Your Ma and him, they had a special kinda' relationship right from the beginnin'. Galen was different even before your Mama came along. There was somethin' about him that didn't belong here. He had too much of the wanderin' waters in him."

"Wandering waters?"

Dutch nodded a private laugh. "Yeah, you wouldn't know that. An old song, one folks was singin' long before there was a town here. 'Everyone knows about wanderin' waters, always keep movin' an' never stay long.' That was your dad. It weren't like he was too good for the place. I don't want you t'think that. Weren't nothin' about your dad that was the least bit arrogant. He didn't put on no airs, but he coulda' 'cause he was somethin' special. Handsome, too, but I don't think that's what drew your Ma to him."

"She was drawn to him?" Abby asked. "But I thought you said "

"Ain't no one in town who din't love your Ma, but it was like a sisterly kinda' love, or maybe it was just a little hero worshippin'. I ain't even sure if maybe it weren't your dad who brought your Ma to town in the first place. She bein' a Walker an' all, it's the energy that draws her in. An' that was your dad, all good thoughts an' bright light."

"They fell in love?"

"Not at first," Dutch said. "At first, it was like they was two cats stakin' out a territory. There was an attraction, anyone could see that, an' a strong one, too. But it was like they knew their lives'd never be the same if they acted on their feelin's, an' besides, how could they? Molly weren't like us, an' not just 'cause she was what she was. She was an outsider, an' no amount of magic or infatuation could change that. There are just some things that are bred into people, an' one of the things bred into us is we don't trust outsiders."

"But you said…"

"We loved her, sure we did, but she weren't of us. And when she an' your Paw fell in love, everybody in town knew somethin' wrong had happened. Awful wrong. That was why they left… that an' what happened in the mine."

"The mine?"

"The Archer Mine, up yonder, near the Falls," Dutch said, and drained the last of his drink.

"Need me another, Teddy," he called to the bartender.

"Think you've had enough," Teddy replied.

"I'll tell you when I've had enough!"

Teddy shrugged. "Promised Penny I'd watch out after ya'."

Dutch scowled but didn't pursue the issue. He lowered his eyes and continued talking in his hushed voice.

"I don't blame Galen for leavin'," he said. "Sometimes this place is a little… crowded. It's hard t'figure out who y'are if y'gotta' keep playin' the same part your whole life."

"Why don't you leave?" Abigail asked.

Dutch laughed harshly. "An' do what?"

"I don't know, anything."

He shook his head. "I'm forty-eight years old, girlie, I ain't never been nowhere other than this valley. Sometimes your prison is where you sleep best at night."

Abby leaned back a little in her chair. "The mine," she said, "What happened there?"

"The Archer was what kept this valley alive," Dutch said. "Mined coal out of it. Dangerous work, that, but the town made such a stinkin' fortune from it folks took the bad with the good. Gave people the luxury of livin' here without gettin' interrupted by the rest of the world. An' also left it wide open for what came later."

"Which was?"

"You met 'em," he said. "Your Goners was part of what came along after that business in the mine. That an' the Red Witch."

"But what happened in the mine?"

Dutch shrugged. "No one's real sure. Eight miners went in, one miner came out. An' he died near two days later."

"Of what?"

"Fear, near as anyone could tell. Fear from what he seen in them tunnels, an' fear of what he an' the others had opened up."

"What was it?" Abby asked.

"The miner who got out, his name was Teke Wells, he wouldn't say much, or maybe he couldn't. He said they'd dug a new tunnel down off the main shaft, no one ever really knew why, weren't no reason t'do it, but they did. An' Teke said they found a door at the end of the tunnels. Excavated it right outta' the earth, like it had been there all along, just waitin'. Teke said he was at the back of the tunnel, behind the others, when they opened the door."

"What did they find?"

"Somethin' so awful it turned poor Teke's hair bone-white."

"But what was it?"

"Dunno'," Dutch said, and seeing Abby's disappointed expression added, "I don't have all the answers to your questions. Nobody does. Some things is just a mystery. But I do know that strange things started happenin' in Sunset Falls not long after."

"What kinds of things?" Abby asked.

"Things that only happened in the dark, in the woods," Dutch replied. "Folks went missin', then turned up totally drained of their blood, but without no marks on their bodies. Livestock, the same way. That's the reason no one goes out after sunset. 'Til you did, that is."

Abigail turned away, toward the door.

"The other night," she said, "in the woods, what happened there? I saw a bright light, and then I woke up in bed."

"Dunno' that either," Dutch said. "Your Aunt Penny woke me up an' said you both had run off an' we needed t'find you. It was the bright light that showed us where you was. You were pretty deep in the woods. Them Goners had run off by the time we pulled you away."

"You came to get us?" Abby asked.

"You sound surprised," Dutch said. "But I s'pose I would be, too. We ain't been real welcoming to ya'. When your folks left Sunset Falls, they took a lot of us with 'em. I think we're maybe takin' a little bit of that out on you."

"What about the light?"

Dutch shrugged. "Ain't got no idea."

"You talked about a Red Witch," Abby said. "So did the Goners. They said she was a Walker, too, like my mother."

Dutch nodded. "Yeah, she is. Only she's another kind of Walker, a bad kind of Walker."

"What's the difference?"

"You remember I said your Ma was attracted to positive energy?"

"Yeah."

"Well, the Red Witch lives on sadness," he said. "She gets her strength from negative energy. Fear, mostly. An' there's damn sure enough fear in Sunset Falls t'feed her appetite."

"She came here after the door in the mine was opened?"

Dutch nodded. "An' after your Ma left. It's almost like them Walkers leave a scent trail, like a predator stakin' it's territory. The Red Witch caught a whiff of Molly's scent marker an' maybe somethin' else, too, a change in the wind, the smell of our fear. Whatever it was, it brought her here. An' now it's almost like I cain't remember a time when she weren't here."

Abby shook her head. "Why don't you call somebody for help?"

Dutch laughed. "Who would we call? The army? A priest? We already got Reverend Martin, an' he ain't been able to do nothin'. There ain't nobody we can call for help. All we've gotta' do is wait it out. Hope she'll leave 'fore too long. Or maybe…"

Dutch looked furtive, then smiled.

"I ever tell you how much you look like your Ma? That red hair of yours… when it catches the light just right, I swear I was lookin' right at her."

Abigail pushed back her chair and stood up.

"My mother's alive, and I'm going to find her," she said. "I don't know how, but I'm not giving up."

"You ain't gonna' find her, not 'less you ain't afraid of where t'look."

"I'm not afraid."

Dutch shrugged. "We'll see about that."

Abigail turned and walked out of the bar. She let the door slam behind her. Ben was outside, on the bench where she'd left him, and where they'd spent their first afternoon in Sunset Falls.

"What happened?" he asked. "You were gone a long time."

"Something's about to happen here," Abby said. "Something big."

Ben blanched. "Oh no, what?"

"I don't know exactly, only that something's building up."

"How do you know?"

"Those voices I'm hearing?" Abby asked. "My whispers?"

"Yeah."

"They're getting louder."

Chapter Eight
Augustus Dolarhyde

The voices kept Abigail awake. They weren't whispers anymore, but fully formed and intelligible voices.

"…understood what she said, but I was…"

"…dog-legged and close to the bone…"

"…without a doubt the last great man…"

The voices cascaded in on top of themselves; so many that Abby could only pick out a few of the louder ones.

Beside her in his bed, Benjamin snored softly. She was glad he could sleep. It gave her time to mull over what Dutch had told her without the distractions of his questions.

There was obviously a lot Dutch had left out. How had her mom come to Sunset Falls in the first place? How did her parents fall in love? Where were they married? And why, exactly, did they leave? What did the Goners do? Were they the ones who sucked the blood out of the townspeople? Was it even the Goners at all? Was there more to that story? And what was behind the door the miners found? And most importantly, how did she and Benjamin figure into it all? Why would their father allow them to come to Sunset Falls if he knew what was going on? Would he have put them in danger?

Abby felt betrayed, not the least by her father. Had he even known what their mother was? Of course he did, he had to. That meant he knew what was going on in Sunset Falls. So why had he sent Abby and Ben here, of all places, the eye of the storm?

Abigail got up off her bed. The springs squeaked and Ben stirred. She stood still for a moment until he went back to sleep. She was barefoot, and the floor was cold. But there was a fever of heavy thoughts in Abigail's pale brow, and she welcomed the chill.

She walked to the window. It was open, and a cool breeze blew in. The summer was fading. Before long, the days in Sunset Falls would be as cool as the nights.

"Abigail," a voice called. At first it was barely distinguishable from the cacophony in her head.

"Abigail," she heard it again. It came from the woods outside the window.

"Who are you?" she asked. "Show yourself."

There was a rustle in the leaves outside, and then a glowing silver shape emerged.

"Augustus?" she asked. "Augustus Dolarhyde?"

"Come down," he said, "Please. I've abandoned the Goners. I'm on my own now. I think I prefer being lost to their sort of found."

"You come up," Abby replied.

"I can't."

"Why not?"

"The rules of the game," he answered. "I don't understand them myself, but we spirits have certain limitations and, well, this is one of them."

"Where are the Goners now?"

"Looking for you, I suppose," Gus said. "Please, come down. I want to show you something."

Abigail considered this for a long moment. It was quite possibly a trap, and if she went outside the other Goners would leap out at her and finish what they'd tried to do the previous night. But she didn't think that was so. There was something nakedly honest in Augustus, and so she crept downstairs and met him on the edge of the forest. She slipped on her shoes as she walked, but she didn't bother with a jacket. The air felt good.

"I'm glad you came down," Augustus said. His silver form floated on a wisp of vapor.

"What did you want to show me?" Abby asked.

The spirit lowered his eyes. "I wish you wouldn't blame me for what happened with the others."

"You were all going to kill me, weren't you?"

"The others were, yes."

"What were you going to do, stand heroically off to the side?"

"I'm not one of them anymore."

"Well, *that's* reassuring," Abby scoffed. "At least Augustus Dolarhyde doesn't want to kill me anymore."

"Please call me Gus," he said.

"Why should I call you anything?"

"Because I'm not like them," Gus replied. "And because I think you're, well…"

"Yes?"

"I think you're the most beautiful person I've ever seen," he said, and lowered his eyes.

Abby raised her eyebrows and stifled a laugh. "That's about the last thing in the world I thought you were going to say."

"It's true."

"You're dead."

"I can still see."

They stood awkwardly in front of the woods, the child of a Walker and a floating silver spirit.

"Thank you, I guess," Abby said hesitantly. "That's nice to say."

"Will you come with me?" Gus asked.

"Where?"

"I really do want to show you something."

"What?"

Gus sighed, exasperated. "Just come with me. It's worth it. Please."

Despite the warnings screaming up from her own logical mind, despite reason wailing at her that it was some sort of set-up, she followed Gus into the woods. There was no moon, but the silver glow of Gus' body provided enough light to see where she was going.

"You said you were the youngest Goner," Abby said. "What does that mean? Baby Millie looked much younger than you. She was just a little kid."

"She was, when she died," Gus replied. "But she died a hundred years ago. I died three."

"Who were you?" Abby asked. "I mean, before you died? Where did you live? Who misses you? Do you have a family?"

"Yes, I have a family. They still live on a farm in Nebraska. We were lucky enough to have a deep well on our land, with enough water to at least keep a field or two growing. I was one summer away from going off to college."

"College? Really?"

"I was smart enough to go, at least that's what the teacher said. Mr. Arkin, his name was. He sat down with my parents at our big kitchen table and told 'em I wasn't meant to stay on the farm, that there were bigger things for me. Said he could arrange it so I could go to university for free up in Lincoln, at the state school. My dad, he was uneasy with it, no one in his family had ever been to college. But he let me go."

"Did you, um, did you die there, at college?" Abby asked.

Gus shook his head. "Three weeks before I was supposed t'go, we were havin' some trouble with our thresher. Big machine, sharp blades, used t'pull the grain off the stalks. The thing started up all of a sudden and in I fell."

"But you look perfectly fine."

"That's another of those rules of the game," Gus replied. "Except that's one I don't mind following. We don't carry our wounds with us."

"But Baby Millie' hair…"

"Afterwards," Gus said. "She picked up that habit, pulling her hair out, after she died."

They walked along in silence. A cool breeze rustled the leaves around them.

"Did you have a girlfriend back in Nebraska?" Abigail asked.

Gus smiled to himself. "No, I didn't."

"Hmm, I thought you might have."

Gus was about to reply when they stepped into a clearing. Abigail gasped.

"This is it," Gus said.

The sound of the waterfall had been drowned out by the ever-present voices, but now, standing in front of it, the roar of the water obliterated all the other sounds.

Abigail stared in awe at Sunset Falls. They cascaded thunderously a hundred feet down the side of the valley wall. Wet rocks at the base broke the water's fall, sending up a fountain of water so dense it was mist. A fast-flowing stream began at the base of the falls and disappeared into the dense woods beyond.

Abby followed Gus to a large, flat rock beside the falls. Together they sat, Gus an inch off the rock's surface, and stared at the water.

"There aren't many places like this here," Gus said. "Sunset Falls is so consumed with fear that it's hard to find somewhere you don't feel it."

"Why isn't this place like the rest of it?" Abby asked.

"This is neutral ground," Gus replied. "A safe haven. A place where nature's power overwhelms man's. Even dead man's."

"I feel calm here."

"Me, too."

Abby closed her eyes. "I haven't felt calm in a long time."

Gus smiled. "I didn't know your mother," he said, "but she must've been remarkable."

"I didn't know her, either," Abby replied. "Not really. I wish she'd told me everything."

"Maybe she would have, in time," Gus said. "Or maybe she

thought you'd be safer if you never knew."

"If I never knew the truth?"

"Look how the truth has made you feel," he said. "You're miserable and confused."

"But at least I know."

Gus shrugged, but didn't answer.

"I can't stay here," Abby said.

"Why not? You're safe here."

"My brother needs me, and so does my mom."

"I thought that…"

"Thank you for showing me this," Abby said, "but it's not real. Yes, it's a real place, I know that, but it's not a real alternative to doing what I know has to be done."

"Which is?"

"Finding my mother."

Gus threw up his transparent hands. "But don't you see, you can't do that."

"Why not?"

"Because they won't let you."

"Who won't?"

"The Goners, the Red Witch, the people of the town, your aunt and uncle…"

"What did you think I'd do when you showed me this place?"

Abby asked. "Be so moved by it that I'd give up looking for my mother?"

"I want to protect you!"

"Why?" she asked. "Because you like me? You've got a little crush on me? If you like me, then respect me, and respect what I need to do. Don't sock me away somewhere safe just because you're afraid. If there's even a tiny chance that my mother's alive somewhere, don't think for one second that anyone, even a cute dead boy, can keep me away from her."

Abby turned away and headed back into the woods.

"Where are you going?" Gus yelled.

"To get my brother," Abby said. "Then to find my mother."

The calm the falls had afforded her drained away as soon as she stepped into the woods. It was replaced with a feeling of dread more pervasive than at any other time. She thought it might be in contrast to how good she'd just felt, but doubted that. Something was happening, and it would happen soon.

They surrounded her before she could sense them. The Goners, four of them now, formed a tight circle around Abigail. Baby Millie screamed, and Abby covered her ears.

"This time, your luck is up," Alice hissed. "I don't know what kind of wizardry you conjured last time, but we won't underestimate you again."

The Goners reached out to Abby. The instant their silver hands touched her skin she was wracked with a burning pain. Abigail felt her life being sucked out through her skin. The power in the Goners' hands overwhelmed her. She remembered what Dutch had said about the blood being drained from peoples' bodies with no marks left and thought she now knew how they did it. The clearing glowed with the Goners' silver light. The less there was of Abigail, the brighter the Goners burned. Abby felt her consciousness slipping away, and then as soon as quickly as it began the burning was gone.

There was a ruckus, leaves falling and tree branches snapping, and Abby shook her head to focus.

Gus had his hands around Alice's thick throat and was holding her tightly. Her eyes bulged unpleasantly and her tongue lolled to one side.

"I won't let you hurt her!" Gus shouted.

"You're a fool!" Alice spat.

Baby Millie shrieked again, which broke Abraham out of his trance. The muscular black man grabbed Gus and tried to pull him away. Gus was strong, and had a strong grip on Alice.

Abigail got to her feet. She stumbled weakly into the woods, not sure where she was going. Something heavy hit her on the head, and blackness abruptly fell.

Chapter Nine

The Witch's Cabin

There was a fire—she felt its warmth on her cheek. She tried to open her eyes. Her head hurt too much, and opening her eyes just didn't seem worth the effort. Abigail was warm even though all she wore was her nightgown. She wondered where she was, but the thought, like everything else, seemed distant and unimportant.

"I hit her too hard." It was Dutch, but a fuzzy version of his voice.

"She's stronger than you realize," a woman replied. She had a small voice, kindly, with a hint of an accent Abby had never heard before.

"She ain't gonna' wake up," Dutch said. "I kilt her, din't I?"

"She's awake now."

Abby opened her eyes. The firelight she'd felt on her face was bright and she turned her head away. She groaned as a wave of pain ran up her neck.

"So, this is the Walker's child," the woman said. Abigail turned to face her. The woman stood behind her, and it took nearly everything Abby had to roll over.

The Red Witch was almost as round as she was short. She had long black hair tied in a single braid. Her clothes were simple, colorless and plain. Her face was moon-shaped. She was an American Indian, with a sharp nose and wide, almost Asian features.

"I've seen you before," Abby said. "You were on the bus."

"I do get around," the Witch replied.

"You're a Walker?"

The Red Witch nodded. "Like your mother."

Abigail struggled to sit up. Her head was muddy, and she thought for a moment she might throw up. She steadied herself and looked around.

Uncle Dutch was in the corner with his tattered brown hat held tight in his worrying hand. They were inside a cabin, small and nondescript. A couple of chairs in front of the fire, a table and chairs behind them, windows painted black with the night—and the fire itself, warmth that now seemed too cloying in the tiny room.

"A little harder next time, Uncle Dutch," Abby said. "I think I still have a few of my teeth left."

Dutch scowled half-heartedly, and lowered his eyes. The Red Witch laughed.

"The cat has claws," she said. "Marvelous."

Slowly, painfully, Abigail got to her feet. She wore only her shoes and nightgown. Under other circumstances, she would have blushed with modesty. Now, well, these weren't other circumstances.

"Where are my manners?" the Witch asked. "Come, child, sit yourself down a spell."

The Witch laughed. "Get it? A spell? Red Witch?" She shook her head. "No one appreciates me."

"I brought her to you," Dutch said.

"So I see," the Red Witch replied. "What, exactly, were you hoping I would do with her?"

"Her mother," Dutch said. "She's still alive."

The Red Witch's expression darkened. "Who said that?"

"The ghosts told her," Dutch replied. "Them Goners said it."

The Witch nodded, and looked up at the upright Abigail. "I see. What else did they talk about?"

"Use your magic powers to find out," Abby replied.

The Red Witch shook her head and smiled. "I think you've been misinformed about me, child Walker. The Red Witch moniker they've given to me? Not my idea. I'm not a witch any more than you are one of those irritating Goners."

"But you're a Walker."

"Walkers and witches, not the same thing," she replied. "Witches are what they are by choice. It's a belief system. You and me, we're acts of nature."

"It's true, then?" Abby asked. "My mother's alive?"

The Walker shrugged. "In the way that any of us Walkers are alive, then, yes, she is."

"What does that mean?" Abby fumed. "I'm tired of riddles and innuendo."

"So you want absolutes?" the Witch laughed. "Then you're in for a lifetime of disappointment."

"I want to know the truth."

"Whose truth?"

Abby threw up her hands. "That's what I mean. Ever since I got here it's been one bit of mumbo-jumbo after another."

"Then you're not paying attention," the Witch said.

"What about Molly?" Dutch asked.

"What about her?" the Red Witch replied.

"I brought you the girl," Dutch said. "I wanna' trade her for her mother."

"What?" Abby spun around to face her uncle. He glanced at her nervously, then back at the Witch.

"And what makes you think I can make such a trade?" the Red Witch asked. She had a mirthful look on her face that Abby couldn't read. Something was going on she didn't understand, some undercurrent she was missing.

"You know why," Dutch said.

"You gave me that Walker in the first place," the Red Witch said. "Now you've changed your mind?"

"I was tricked," Dutch said. "You tricked me. I never gave her to you."

"You handed her over to me in exchange for peace in your town."

"And you stayed here anyway!" Dutch flared.

The Witch smiled. "You're a bad negotiator."

"If I knew you wouldn't leave, I never would have - -"

"What did you do?" Abby shouted, and flung herself at Dutch. The unexpected force of her attack took him by surprise, and he fell to the floor. Abigail rained blows down upon him, furious blows he couldn't (or wouldn't) block.

"I loved her, Abigail, you gotta' unnerstan' that," Dutch said.

"What did you do?" Abby asked again. She punched Dutch hard on the cheeks and chest. He didn't resist.

"She tricked me, I never woulda' done it if - -" But before Dutch could finish, Abigail was lifted off him by an unseen hand, and flung hard against the far wall. She landed in a heap, winded.

"Enough of this!" the Witch bellowed. The fire in the fireplace flared and for a moment the Witch seemed a dozen feet tall. Then her anger ebbed and the room returned to normal.

"Dutch Crosley, you are a spineless coward," the Witch said. "And you are a fool. You handed me the Walker, and now you've brought me her offspring. And you will get nothing from me. I have spared your town the worst of what haunts it - -"

"But it's worse than it's ever - -"

"- - and I will continue to do so. You're more useful to me when you cower in your homes, anyway. But with this half-child, I can achieve something no Walker has ever done… complete immersion."

"What are you talking about?" Abigail asked. She pulled herself up against the wall on wobbly legs.

"You have no idea what we are, do you?" the Witch asked. "The incredible gifts we have?"

"What are you - -?"

"The voices you hear, the ones that grow louder and more distinct every day?"

"How do you know about that?"

"I hear them, too. It's a Walker trait. Part of our cursed existence."

Abigail shook her head to clear it. "What are they, then, that we're hearing?"

"Other worlds," the Witch said. "Other dimensions, planes of existence, whatever you want to call them. They are worlds that exist parallel to our own. And they are ripe with such delicious fear."

"You're insane," Abby said.

"Not yet, dear, just hungry."

"But how do I - -?"

"You're a bridge," the Witch said. "A most rare of creatures, so rare, in fact, that no other has existed for a millennia. A half-breed child, capable of breaching the walls of the other worlds and immersing yourself within them. Walking, as it were, anywhere you want to go."

Abigail stood against the cabin wall, letting the words sink in. Other worlds… she couldn't imagine it. Was that what she'd been hearing? Voices from parallel worlds?

"Give me back my Molly!" Dutch whimpered. "Please."

The Red Witch whirled around to face him.

"Quit your whining, Dutch Crosley," she said. "I don't know where she is."

"But you took her!"

"I didn't keep her," the Witch replied. "What use do I have for another Walker? I sent her away."

"Where?" Dutch asked.

"Who knows? Hard to tell, really. 'Away' can be so many places."

Abigail stood up. The pain in her head, and the pain of being tossed about had both vanished. In their place was a calm, blue fury.

"Where is my mother?" she asked.

For the first time since Abby had awakened in the cabin, the Red Witch looked shaken. Her unflappable confidence seemed flapped, at least a little. Her smile left her face and she took a step backwards.

"Forget about her," the Witch said. "She's gone too far away."

"I can go anywhere," Abby replied. "You said so yourself."

The Red Witch now looked genuinely squeamish. Abby felt her newfound calm cascade through her body, down her arms and out her fingers.

"You can't go anywhere unless you know how," the Witch said. "And there's no one here but me to show you how to do it."

"Then show me."

The Witch laughed, but it was half-hearted.

"What kind of bargain is that?" she asked. "I tell you what to do, you go find your mother, and then I have to leave?"

"Why would you have to leave?" Abby asked.

"Rules of the game, just like the voices. Part of the whole rotten thing. Can't be two Walkers in one place. Throws off the balance. Gums up the works. It's just not allowed."

"Says who?"

"What do you mean, says who? Says the way it is, says the way it's always been. Those are the rules, and that's how it's played."

"So what do you want?" Abigail asked. "You must want something. Bargain with me."

"You know what I want," the Witch hissed.

Abby nodded. "Complete immersion."

The Witch scowled. "You don't know what you've gotten yourself into, little girl."

"So tell me!" Abby exclaimed. As her frustration got the better of her, a feeling like rushing floodwaters overtook her body. For a moment she felt like she was drowning beneath it. Before panic could set in, however, the sensation left her, radiating out like a blast from her body. The shock wave knocked Dutch and the Red Witch off their feet. The table and all the chairs went flying. Embers from the fire blew out onto the floor, smoldering on the bare wood.

For a long, pregnant moment, there was silence. Even the ever-present voices had stopped. Then slowly, softly, the voices began again and Abigail realized her moment had almost passed.

Without looking at either Dutch or the Witch, Abby bolted for the door. She pushed it open and felt the cool rush of night air. It was now or never—whatever had happened, whatever she had done, it had afforded her one chance to get away. And Abby wasn't foolish enough to let it pass.

Abigail fled from the Red Witch's cabin into the woods. She didn't know where she was going, but she knew she had to stay near Sunset Falls. The answers to everything, who she was, where she came from, even where her mother was, they were all there. All she had to do was find them.

Chapter Ten

Huckleberry Browntree

At first, she thought it was the same cabin. In the dark, in the woods, it would have been easy enough to run around in circles. But this cabin was larger, and lamps burned in the windows. In the darkness, she didn't know where she was. She hadn't run far—definitely not out of the valley. Abby knew the Goners were close by. She'd sensed them all around her. They hadn't found her yet, but would. And when they did, even after what she'd done at the Witch's cabin, Abby knew she wouldn't last long.

Abigail rapped on the wooden door. For a moment there was no sound, and she felt she might have to turn into Goldilocks and break in. But then softly from the other side of the door a man spoke.

"Go away."

"Hello?" Abby called. "Please let me in."

"You one of them?"

"No, I'm not."

"How would you know what I'm talking about if you weren't one?"

"Because *they're* following *me*," Abby replied.

There was silence again, then the sound of a massive series of locks being turned. The sound was out of place in the middle of the woods. It sounded like a bank vault opening instead of the door of an isolated cabin. The door opened and warm light spilled out into the night. A large hand grabbed Abigail's sleeve and pulled her inside. The door closed behind her, and the locks were turned again.

The cabin was larger than the Red Witch's, but not nearly as large as Dutch and Penny's house. There were three rooms, a main living room, a bedroom and another room, dark. The place was crowded floor to ceiling with machines of every imaginable description. Bottles and tubes were scattered among them, some attached by long hoses, some filled with bubbling liquids. There were beakers and test tubes and even a large microscope, and in the center of it all, his long hair flowing behind him, was the man who'd let her in.

He had thick glasses attached around his head like goggles. They in fact reminded Abby of the kind of eyepieces pilots wore. His hair was longer than any man's she'd ever seen, past his shoulders and on its way down his back. He wore thick leather gloves and a stained white smock. After he locked the door, it was as if he didn't even remember Abby was in the room. He turned a series of cranks on the nearest machine, a barrel-shaped contraption that rumbled and belched to life.

"Thank you," Abigail said. The man glanced past her, and as if suddenly realizing what she'd said, made a two-fingered salute off the corner of his forehead.

"You're not one of them," he said, as if that explained everything. Then he disappeared behind another machine, larger than the other and with octopus arms of piping leading to other machines and beakers. Abby stepped toward the machine, and peered around.

"My name's Abigail," she said as he popped his head up. "Abigail Crosley."

"Okay," he shrugged.

Abby was confused. "You let me in," she said. "I thought maybe you'd want to know who I was."

The man in goggles didn't say anything, simply moved along a line of beakers, each with its own uniquely colored liquid, red, blue, green, tangerine...

"I've seen you," Abby said. "Well, *saw* you is actually what I mean. The first day I came here, in town. You were walking out of the general store."

"Miss, I would very much like to get acquainted," the man said, "but those things outside will be making their nightly attempt to get inside. And since they're following you, as you explained, I can only imagine they will be especially persistent."

"Fair enough," Abby replied. "But could you at least tell me who you are?"

The man sighed and walked through the dangling machinery toward Abigail. He extended his hand, then, remembering his manners, took off his glove.

"Huckleberry Browntree," he said, then when there was no reaction from Abby, added, "*The* Huckleberry Browntree."

"I can't imagine there'd be more than one of you," Abby quipped.

"You haven't heard of me," Huckleberry Browntree said matter-of-factly. "Not that it's a surprise. I mean, the best of us toil most of our lives in obscurity."

"I'm sorry," Abby said. "*Should* I know you?"

"No surprise at all," Browntree continued, as if not hearing her. "No big discoveries. Ever since penicillin, it's all theater. Hard to appreciate real science when there are so many show ponies hawking miracle elixirs."

"You're a scientist, then?"

"Yes, a scientist," Browntree replied. "Not that anyone notices. Took all the government money I could scrounge to get here. They think I'm developing a new process to leach coal. Imagine! And this equipment… borrowed money, mostly, although they will be missing it by now. Essential, though. Wouldn't have lasted long without it."

"What is all this?"

Browntree continued to turn knobs and adjust dials as he spoke.

"Electronometers, magnetoscopes, an ossmonitor, a transosmetrophone for decoding and translating electric impulse readings, and this big one is the electromagnetic burst generator."

Another machine kicked to life, adding its rhythmic KA-CHUNK, KA-CHUNK to the cacophony of noise. Browntree peered at Abby around the corner of the electromagnetic burst generator.

"It's like I'm speaking Greek to a Roman, isn't it?" he said.

"I understand what you said," Abby replied. "I'm just not sure what all this is for."

"Study."

"Of what?"

"Of those things out there." He stepped around the machine and took both his gloves off.

"The Goners," Abigail said.

Browntree looked at her more closely. "You're that girl from the woods."

"I ran through the woods to get here, but - -"

"No, no, the other night, when they were particularly rambunctious. I wasn't sure if the electromagnetic burst generator would do the trick."

"The white light," Abby said. "That was you?"

An enormous grin erupted on Browntree's face. "That's wonderful news! You made it! Do you realize what this means? It *does* work!"

"Yeah, it does," Abby replied, "but what exactly does it do?"

Browntree shook his bushy head as if he were attempting to settle on a starting point to his explanation.

"It's a burst of highly-concentrated static electricity," he said, excited. "My theory was, and the magnetometers confirmed it, is that those things, those… what did you call them?"

"Goners."

"Goners, fine. Well, I was able to discover that they are comprised almost entirely of a volatile electrical charge. I thought that if I could disrupt their current, I could disrupt them."

"And that's what your burst machine did?"

Browntree frowned. "Yes, that's what my 'burst machine' did."

"But what about the - -?" Abby began, but was cut off by the loud metallic TICK-TICK-TICK of another machine.

"What's that?" she asked.

Huckleberry Browntree's face went pale.

"They're here," he said.

Several other machines began making noises, and a beaker of blue liquid started to bubble. Steam belched from the top of a round stovepipe attached to a square metal box. Browntree turned a series of knobs, but the steam didn't let up.

"They're definitely here, all right," he said. "Stronger, too, this time. They're making the electroanalagizer go haywire. That steam? It shouldn't be happening."

"Are we safe in here?" Abby asked.

"Safer than out there."

"But will they get in?"

Browntree shook his head. "Not possible."

As if hearing a challenge in his words, the walls of the cabin shook like they'd been hit by something heavy. Dust fell from the ceiling. For the first time since Abby had met him, Browntree didn't have anything to say. They both stared at the ceiling, then at the front door.

Another vibration shook the cabin. This time they saw the door move inward. More dust fell, and the machines continued to belch frantically.

"We need to get out of here," Browntree said.

"But I thought you said - -"

"I know what I said, and I've changed my hypothesis," he snapped. "I don't know what they want with you, but you've definitely got them in an uproar."

"Where are we going to go?" Abigail asked.

"I know a place," Browntree said. "I don't think they'll look there. I don't think they can."

"Where?"

"The mines," he said. "They avoid them. I don't know why."

"We can't go into the mines," Abby said.

"Why not?"

"There are bad things in there, *very* bad things. It's why all of this is happening now."

Browntree began filling a knapsack with smaller machines, box-shaped contraptions with dials and switches. He slung the pack over his shoulder and picked up a flashlight from a nearby table.

"Young lady, we have two options," he said. "One is stay here where we are certain of our outcome, and the other is go to the mines where, aside from the threat of some folksy local ghost tales, our chances are much greater that we'll get to see another sunrise."

"Look, you don't understand what you're - -"

"I would very much not to have to leave you here, but I will if you don't hurry."

They stared each other down like two prizefighters, and then Abigail let out a frustrated growl.

"All right, let's go."

Huckleberry Browntree bent down and opened a trap door in the floor. A set of steep wooden steps led to a dark tunnel. Browntree turned on the flashlight and climbed down. Abby followed him. He closed the door above their heads, and the rumble of the machines grew distant.

They were in a tunnel, wide and tall enough for them to walk through. The walls were crudely cut from the earth. In places, roots poked through. They were under the forest, maybe two dozen feet below. The air was cool and close.

"What is this place?" Abby asked.

"Plan B," Browntree replied. "Only I didn't think I'd actually need to use it. But isn't that always the way with a Plan B?"

"You mean this leads to the mines?"

"Near enough," he said. "The Goners' electromagnetic awareness has trouble penetrating through the ground. I'm not sure why. But they can't sense we're down here. It gives us the few minutes head start we'll need."

"What about all your machinery?" Abby asked.

Browntree sighed. "Yes, well, I suppose they'll destroy it out of spite. They're awfully angry, aren't they? I can't quite figure out why."

"They're trapped," Abigail replied. "Between this world and another. They want to move on, I think."

"That's no excuse."

"No, but it's a reason."

They came to the end of the tunnel. It was another trap door like in Browntree's cabin, except this one was directly in front of them, not over their heads. Browntree turned off the flashlight and opened the door. They emerged from the side of a hill, facing the entrance to the Archer Mine. A decrepit wooden sign proclaimed it as such, and a dark tunnel led into the Appalachian foothill behind it. They were at the edge of the valley.

"My poor little cabin," Browntree lamented. Abby followed his gaze.

Behind them, through the trees, a silver glow illuminated the forest. It was as if the moon was setting directly in the middle of it. Abby heard Baby Millie's shrill laugh and shuddered. Wood splintered in the distance. Machinery was toppled. They had gotten inside Browntree's cabin.

"That would've been us," Abby said.

"And it still could," Browntree replied, shaking himself from his reverie. "Come on, they'll realize what's happened before too long. The female of them is a bit of a whip."

"Alice."

Browntree shook his head. "I'm still marveling at the fact that they didn't kill you."

Abby shrugged. "My mother was a strong woman."

"What's that supposed to - -?"

"We'll have a long talk about everything, but I think now you're right about getting into the mine."

Browntree slung his pack higher on his shoulder. They walked the last dozen feet from the trap door to the mine. He turned the flashlight on, and together they disappeared down the abandoned shaft.

Chapter Eleven

Dutch and Penny

Benjamin watched the sun come up from under his bed. He couldn't believe she'd done this to him... not again, and not without warning. Didn't Abby realize how much he needed her, especially after he followed her into the forest?

He wiped tears out of his eyes. He wouldn't cry anymore. He was too old for that. Besides, what had crying ever gotten him? Absolutely nothing. Even if he cried his eyes out, he'd still be in the same predicament afterwards. Abigail was gone, and he hadn't been able to stop her.

Ben realized for the first time that he was alone with Uncle Dutch and Aunt Penny. No, Abigail wouldn't do that to him, not for real. And not for long. She'd be back, she'd...

But he knew that wasn't going to be, not this time. She was really gone, and all the bad-to-worse scenarios he could imagine were about to come true.

The house had been quiet for a long time. After they'd discovered her gone, Dutch and Penny had left the house to look for her. Ben thought he should go, too, but he was much too afraid. He decided hiding under the bed was his best move, and that's where he'd stayed. Only now, after the slamming of the kitchen door and Uncle Dutch's angry footsteps on the stairs, did he realize he'd made a big mistake.

"Don't hurt the boy, y'big fool, he's all we got now," Penny called.

"He knows where she is," Dutch said. He thundered up the stairs, and in a moment was standing in the doorway of the attic bedroom. His ragged breathing was loud in the silence.

"Boy, you better come out now," Uncle Dutch said. "So help me, I ain't in the mood for no games."

Ben pulled himself into a tight ball. His heart pounded frantically. He could smell the rage coming off Dutch like sweat.

"He don't know nothin'," Penny said. She was behind him now in the doorway—Ben saw both sets of their shoes from his vantage point.

"He *do* know," Dutch replied. "He an' that sister of his never did nothin' apart."

Dutch flung open the closet door. There was nothing in it and Dutch turned to face Ben's bed.

"Last chance, boy," he said.

Ben didn't move. He *couldn't* move, his fear was so intense. Dutch's heavy boots clamped closer to the bed. Ben gasped. Dutch picked up the bed and lifted it up. He let it fall to one side. Ben was curled up, trembling, now completely in the open. Dutch picked him up by the shoulders.

"Where is she?" he roared.

Ben couldn't answer him. He wanted to, but he had no control over his voice. Dutch shook him.

"Your sister, boy. Where'd she go?"

"I don't know!" Ben cried out at last.

"Liar!"

"Honest, I don't know!" Ben wept. "I was asleep an' when I got up she was already gone. I swear!"

"He ain't lyin', Dutch," Penny said. She spoke so calmly that even Dutch looked over at her.

"How d'you know?" he asked.

"Why would he still be here?" she replied. "He went after her the last time she left, why wouldn't he do it again? No, this boy's been left behind."

Dutch and Ben were both surprised at Penny's words. Dutch looked down at Ben with disgust, then tossed him onto Abigail's bed. He landed with a thud on the uncomfortable mattress.

"You ain't even worth the trouble," Dutch scoffed.

"Enough!" Penny said. "This boy ain't your trouble. An' neither is his sister. It's that witch in the woods. You an' them other men, you made a mistake when you made your deal with her. Now you gotta' solve it, not this boy, and not even Abigail."

"Don't talk about this in front of him!" Dutch exclaimed.

"Too late for secrets now, Dutch," Penny said. "You gotta' solve this problem 'fore it gets worse. You an' them other men, not some children."

"But she's a - -"

"I don't care what she is, she ain't here t'solve our problems. She ain't one of us, an' she never will be. I don't care if she's your brother's blood, she still ain't what's gonna' save this town."

"Then what is?" Dutch asked. "Me? You? Ain't no one else who can do it."

"And ain't one of us gonna'," Penny retorted. "*All* of us is gonna' do it. That's how it's gotta' be. This town ain't just one person, or two people. It's everybody together. That's how we gotten through everything before. That's how we're gonna' get through this."

Dutch scowled. "You always been a naïve fool."

Penny shrugged, unaffected by her husband's insult.

"Naïve, maybe," she said, "but never a fool. I been played for one, a'course, but only by you. And only for a short time. I'm smarter'n you give me credit for, Dutch, an' that's where you always make your mistakes."

"Sometimes I wonder where the real witch lives, here or in the woods."

Penny smiled, revealing her tiny, yellow teeth.

"That's the funny thing 'about bein' surrounded by so much power, ain't it?" she asked. "Only by the illuminatin' light of it do you finally realize how insignificant you really are."

Dutch had heard enough. He spun around and angled his broad frame through the small attic doorway. He pounded down the stairs and slammed the door on his way out.

Ben started to tremble. He began to realize that Dutch and all his threatening bulk were preferable to the grinning yellow teeth of his aunt.

"Your Mama was a plague on this town," she said. "She batted her pretty blue eyes an' worked whatever kinna' magic she did, an' the whole town was taken in. But not me. No, I saw Molly Walker for what she was. A vulture, nothin' more. A wild dog that strayed from its pack, lookin' for the next carcass to feast on. And we all was fit to be feasted on. So full of our own self-righteous pride, sittin' pretty in front of God an' the whole world with a mine full of coal an' a town of strong-backed men an' God-fearin' women, we was near bustin' with good times. And your Mama smelled that, an' followed the scent 'til she landed smack dab in the middle of Sunset Falls, West Virginia. Every man who cast his eyes on her fell in love with her. The women, too—they saw her as a sister, a friend, someone they wanted t'know.

But I saw her for what she was right from the start. I could smell her evil just like she could smell our happiness. Nobody believed me, a'course, 'cause their eyes was glossed over. I knew it, though, an' I knew it was only a matter of time 'fore everyone else woke up. They did, too, 'cept by then it was a long way past too late. Them fool miners had opened the door an' let the nasty things out. Then the mine closed, an' Sunset Falls weren't such a happy place t'be no more. So your Mama left, an' she took ol' Galen with her. An' Sunset Falls became a kinna' hell on earth."

Aunt Penny stepped over to the window and stared down at the yard below. Benjamin looked at her as if for the first time. She wasn't nearly as physically menacing as he'd thought, not even much taller than him. But even from the back he sensed a tightness about her, a reptilian coil that gave the impression, even in repose that she could strike without warning. She was always right, too, or believed she was, but the difference between the two was inconsequential. If Aunt Penny believed it, it was so. It was that combination of high-strung righteousness that made her dangerous.

"But despite what she was, an' despite what she did, I don't blame her for it," Penny said. "Same as I don't blame a plague of disease for wipin' out the people I care about. Ain't the disease's fault, it just does what it does. Your Mama was a parasite, an' she found some very willin' hosts."

"My mother wasn't a disease," Benjamin said, furious.

"You knew her so good, then, did ya'?" Penny asked. "You knew all about her? You din't even know she was a Walker. 'Sides, children only see the part of their parents they want to see. Ain't possible for 'em to see more'n that. Like lookin' at one of them drawin' puzzles, the kind where there's a face an' a vase an' you can only see one of them things at a time? An' your Mama kept herself hid. Takin' a mortal man as her husband, an' then livin' among regular folk, she had no choice."

Aunt Penny turned around again. She had her back to the window, and rested her hands on the wooden sill. For a moment, Ben thought he could push her out. Penny would crash through the glass, screaming and scared, and land in a jumble of broken neck and twisted limbs on the ground below. But even as he thought it he knew he'd never do it. He was too afraid. Fear was his curse, and it was what immobilized him now.

"Your sister is her Mama's child," Penny said. "She got enough of her father in her t'keep her feet on the ground, but I can see Molly in there, too, in every movement Abigail makes. The way she walks, the way she carries herself—even the fire-red of her hair. But she ain't like Molly in one great big way."

"What's that?"

"Your sister's angry. That's the difference. Your sister, she got a fury in her belly that burns hotter'n any I ever seen. Your Mama di'n't have that. Molly, she was calm an' smilin'. Always smilin'. Maybe it's what happens when you start mixin' up our kind an' their kind. All the ingredients work t'gether 'cept one. There's a reason why heaven's set up away from us. Gods and men ain't s'pposed t'mix. Your Mama made a mistake when she fell in love with a regular man. Maybe she even realized it, there at the end."

"Why do you hate us so much?" Ben asked. "Is it because we left town? Is it because my mother and father were happy with each other?"

"You don't unnerstan' nothin', do ya', boy?"

"I think I understand a whole lot," Ben stood up, buoyed by his anger.

"I've never seen a group of people so afraid of everything," he said. "And you're the center of it. You an' Uncle Dutch. You snap at each other like angry dogs, and then you wonder why you're unhappy. My mother didn't do this to you; all she did was shine a light on your own sadness. She was happy, and my dad was happy, and that's what you hated. Maybe you thought it took something away from you, by them being happy. You're wrong. All your own unhappiness, you brought it on yourself. You an' your whole town. You wallow around in self-pity like pigs. That's why your Red Witch came, and that's why the Goners are - -"

"That's enough!" Penny roared. "That's all I'm gonna' hear outta' you. You got some of your sister's insolence. But one problem child at a time. We'll find your sister, then we'll see what we're gonna' do with you."

Penny strode past Benjamin, her small body looming large over him. When she got to the door, she turned to face him.

"I see how afraid you are," she said, then smiled a crocodile's grin. "You got good reason t'be."

And then she left, and Ben was alone, truly alone, for the first time in his life.

Chapter Twelve

Last Goner Standing

Benjamin hated the outhouse. He hated both the idea and the reality of it. It smelled like stale poo, and it was a long walk from the house. But when he had to go, he had to go, and boy, did he have to go.

It was dark, well after midnight. He'd tiptoed past Dutch and Penny's room, down the stairs and out the door and here he was, pajamas around his ankles and his eyes straight ahead.

A crescent moon shape was cut into the wooden door, affording Ben a slim view of the outside. The moon was bright, not full but nearly so. Ben could see a sliver of the woods through the hole. Leaves blew in a gentle breeze. Ben sighed and shook his head.

He remembered a night in New York, not long before his dad was out of work the first time. It had been a night like this, calm but buzzing in the way only New York could be after dark. Dad had wakened them all, Abby and Ben and even Mom, and together they'd scaled the fire escape to the roof of their building. Dad had a blanket set out, and some lemonade. It was August and the blistering heat had given way to a bathtub-warm night. The family lay down together on the roof and Dad pointed to the sky. At first they couldn't see anything, then slowly as their eyes got accustomed to the city's glow, lights began to appear in the sky. They flashed for only a moment, as quick as a blink, but Ben knew they were really there.

"It's the meteor shower," his dad had said. "Used t'see 'em every year back home. My brother an' me, we used t'sneak out after midnight, after the moon went down, an' stare up at the meteors. Dutch used t'call 'em the dancin' lights. We could see 'em real good, too, since there weren't no other lights. Not like here, where the city's brighter than the sky."

As much as Abby missed their mother, that's how much Ben missed their dad. He didn't show it—men weren't supposed to show their feelings, that's what his dad had always said. But Ben's feelings were too big to keep inside. Mostly he missed happiness. That was his dad's job. He was fun and kind and strong and gentle, and he was the funniest person Ben had ever known. That's why it hurt so much when his mom died. Ben hadn't just lost her; he had lost his dad, too. They were connected in some way that Ben had never realized before. He'd never seen them apart when Dad wasn't working, and he couldn't imagine it was possible. Whatever his dad did, his mom did, too. When it happened, when his mom died, Ben had lost both of his parents. Ben and Abby hadn't been enough to keep him going, and now they were here, in the middle of nowhere in the worst mess they could imagine. He hated his dad a little... well, more than a little, if truth be told. He hated his dad for giving up, and for leaving them all alone.

Ben finished up. There was no way to flush, so he reached to open the door.

Something moved across the crescent moon hole. Ben shook his head, hoping (praying) that his eyes had fooled him. He stood stock-still. He put his hand on the door.

There, again, a flash of movement. This time a sound, a rustle of tree limbs. Ben's blood froze. If he'd had anything left to pee, it would likely have trickled down his leg. Slowly, reluctantly, he released his hand from the door handle.

The outhouse started to shake. It was gentle at first, then harder and harder until dust fell from the ancient boards. Ben screamed and he yanked open the door. His pajamas were still around his ankles. He tripped and fell headfirst into the dewy grass. The outhouse continued to shake. Ben pulled up his pants and hobbled to his feet. He ran as fast as he could toward the house.

It was on top of him in a moment, flooding him in brilliant silver light. Ben squirmed and crawled and tried to break away. It was stronger than he was, and in a moment he was totally subdued. A silver hand covered his mouth.

"Quit screaming," a male voice said. "I won't hurt you."

Ben struggled to say something. The silver hand moved down to rest on his chin.

"You're one of the Goners," Ben said. "Augustus Dolarhyde."

"Yes, you're right."

Ben screamed again, and Dolarhyde clamped his mouth shut.

"Will you keep quiet? They'll hear you if you keep screaming."

"Who will hear me?" Ben asked. It came out, "moo mill meer me?"

"Alice, Baby Millie," Dolarhyde said. "The rest of the Goners."

He lowered his hand from Ben's mouth.

"But you're with them, aren't you?" Ben asked.

"*Was* with them," Dolarhyde replied. He cocked an eyebrow. "I tendered my resignation."

"You quit?'

"I like to think of it as creative differences," Dolarhyde quipped. "Look, I can trust you not to run if I let you go, right?"

"Why shouldn't I run?"

"You want to help your sister, don't you?"

Ben's eyes grew big. "You've seen my sister?"

Dolarhyde nodded. "Last night. They followed her into the woods, to a cabin where she and some other man, some scientist, I

Sunset Falls

don't know, got away from them."

"Where did she go?"

"The mines, I think," Dolarhyde answered. "Our kind can't go in there. I think the man she's traveling with knew that."

Augustus Dolarhyde pulled Ben to his feet. He himself had no feet, instead floated on a cloud of silver smoke a few inches off the ground. He led Ben into the woods. The ghost's silver glow illuminated a radius around them as they walked.

"Your sister's in some real danger," the spirit said.

Ben went pale. "Okay, Mr. Dolarhyde, give it me straight. I can take it."

Dolarhyde laughed. "First of all, you need to call me Gus. It's a lot less work for your mouth. Second, I wouldn't worry too much about your sister right now. She's probably in the safest place she could be, considering. I mean, unless she's happened to stumble into the Dark Tunnel, but that seems unlikely."

Ben's voice was tiny. "What happens in the Dark Tunnel?"

"If she made it to the end, which would be even less likely, she'd unlock the Final Barrier and, well, we would know if she'd done that."

"How?"

"Because there'd be a great deal more people like me flying around," Gus replied. "The Dark Tunnel leads to a crossover point, a passageway to another dimension."

"A ghost world?" Ben asked.

"In a way, yes, I suppose," Gus said. "But over there, we're not ghosts. At least not in this form. It's like... well, it's like moving to a new town. You don't know the people, everything seems strange, but it's familiar enough that you just kind of carry on. Most of us don't even know we've died. It's only the curious ones, the cursed ones, who figure it out."

"Like you?"

Gus nodded. "Like me."

Ben had more questions, (about a million, truth be told), but before he could form them, he tripped and tumbled head-over-heels down a steep embankment. He cried out.

Ben landed face down in ice-cold water. A creek ran through the woods, and Ben had landed in it. He pulled himself out, dripping wet and shivering. Gus was beside him in a moment, grinning.

"I haven't had to watch my step in so long I forgot that you do," he said.

"It's freezing," Ben cried.

Gus raised a hand. "Keep your voice down. The Goners are on the hunt tonight."

Ben shook himself off, but kept quiet. There was a cool breeze picking up, and he wished for a coat.

"Where are we?" Ben asked.

"Downstream," Gus replied. "The Sunset Falls are just up the hill. This creek is one of several tributaries."

Ben took off his pajama top and wrung it out.

"That's what I miss most, I think," Gus said.

"What is?"

"Water," he replied. "Rain. The feel of it on my skin. In my hair."

"What's it like?" Ben asked. "I mean, being the way you are? Can you feel things?"

"I grabbed you, didn't I?" Gus retorted. "It takes an effort to make physical contact. And there's no sense of warmth, not like it used to be when I'd touch someone. I can feel you, but it's like soft rock, not skin."

"My uncle said you drink blood."

Gus laughed. "No, not blood. The Goners are after spiritual essence. Alice said it gave us strength."

"But you don't believe that."

"No," he replied. "I think there are other ways to get what we need. Your mother's way, for instance."

"You can do that?" Ben asked. "Feed on good energy?"

"Not like a Walker can, no, but we don't need the kind of nourishment they do. Having a physical body requires a great deal of positive energy to sustain. Or negative energy, like the other Walker."

"But what you're - -" Ben asked, but Gus raised an arm to cut him off.

"What's wrong?" Ben whispered.

"They're coming," Gus said. "We've got to hurry."

"Where are we going?"

"The mines, you'll be safe there."

"What about you?"

"I'll manage. Come on!"

Gus led Ben up the creek bank and into the forest. They were on the other side of the creek now. The forest was dense. Heavy undergrowth impeded Ben's progress.

"You've got to hurry," Gus said, floating beside him.

"It's too tangled, I can't move!" Ben's short legs fought against the dense forest floor.

He heard them now, a sound like bats in the trees. Ben's heart raced. Slowly, painfully slowly, he cut his way through the woods. Gus' silver glow illuminated his makeshift path.

The Goners were nearly on top of him. He felt static electricity popping in the air. They were all around him, trying to cut him off. Fear made Ben move faster, and also fury that these things were making him run through dark woods in the middle of the night. He pushed his way past tree limbs and tangled vines until at last he burst from the woods. He took off after Gus in a full run.

"The Walker's son!" the Goner named Alice hissed. She was right behind him. If she could've breathed, he would've felt it on his neck. Instead, the air around him popped like a kind of electrified popcorn storm.

"There's the mineshaft!" Gus called. Ben ran for it, a dark tunnel in the side of an enormous hillside bounded by woods like a picture frame. Despite its darkness, Ben never thought anything looked so inviting.

Ben tripped. He knew he was going down, saw the whole thing in slow motion, but he couldn't stop. His legs went out from under him and he sprawled forward. He rolled over onto his back.

The Goners were on him in a heartbeat. Their silver-blue bodies hovered over him. The one called Alice straddled his small chest. Her eyes burned and she smiled a terrible smile.

"Where there's a Walker's son, a Walker's daughter is sure to follow," Alice said.

"Leave me alone!" Ben cried.

Alice glanced at the two Goners nearest to her, Leopold and Abraham.

"Take care of Augustus," she said. "And make it hurt."

The two male Goners left Ben's periphery. Only Alice remained, with Baby Millie behind her.

"Where is she, boy?" Alice asked softly.

"Who?"

Alice flared, and then regained her composure. "Your sister, fool. Your sister."

"She ran away, I don't know where she - -"

"Liar!" Alice's eyes blazed with a kind of blue flame, and Ben's skin prickled with the electricity in the air.

Alice's cold silver hands locked around his neck. The sensation of them on his skin was like smoke, solid smoke, though, and strong. Ben couldn't breathe.

"Where is the Walker girl?" Alice asked. Her hands tightened. Ben's eyes bulged. He knew he was going to die. He knew it with the kind of certainty he'd rarely felt before. And it wasn't a bad feeling. Quite the contrary—it was peaceful. His consciousness blurred and he felt weightless. He didn't fight it.

Then he was free, and air rushed painfully back into his lungs. Alice was gone. For a moment, he thought he had died. But the pain in his lungs made him doubt that. He rolled over, fighting the urge to vomit. Ben looked up.

Gus and Alice were locked in at what first seemed to be an embrace. Their ghostly arms were wrapped tightly around each other, and their faces were intimately close. Only upon closer inspection could Ben decipher the fury of their struggle.

Gasping for breath and holding his aching neck, Ben clamored to his feet. He was lightheaded, and almost fell down again.

The other Goners, Leopold and Abraham and even Baby Millie, surrounded Gus and Alice. For a moment at least, Ben's way was clear. He didn't need an invitation. Using the last of his strength, he ran headlong toward the mineshaft. Baby Millie saw him go. She let out a shriek. It was too late. Ben slipped into the darkness of the mine, safe for now from the horrible grip of his ghostly pursuers.

Chapter Thirteen

Leap of Faith

"Your name is really Huckleberry?" Abby asked. The man nodded. The light from his flashlight cast a long shadow on the mine wall. "Like the Mark Twain book?"

"I thought I'd heard the last of people making fun of my name when I left grammar school," Browntree replied.

"I'm not making fun, I'm just…"

"It's a family name, if you must know," he said. "Named after my paternal grandfather. I don't believe my parents ever read 'Tom Sawyer'."

"I didn't mean anything by it."

Browntree looked at her, studying her expression. Then, satisfied she was an honest sort, nodded curtly.

"You should get some sleep," he said.

Abby laughed hoarsely. "I couldn't sleep now even if my life depended on it."

"We're safe."

"We're not safe," she said. "Just not in any immediate danger."

Browntree nodded. "Fair enough."

They were quiet for a time. Abigail stared at Browntree's trembling reflection against the mine wall.

"Do you believe in God?" she asked.

"Which one?" he replied.

"Is there more than one?"

"Take your pick," he replied. "Every culture has their version. Jehovah or Allah or Krishna or Zeus. Sometimes even more than one."

"You don't believe in it, then?"

"Does it matter?" he asked, and sighed. "I think people spend so much time figuring out what to call it that they miss out on appreciating the mystery of it."

"But isn't that what you're doing?" Abigail asked. "With your machines and your experiments? Figuring it out?"

"I don't claim to know the answers," he said. "And no amount of investigation will ever tell me."

"So what are you doing, then?"

"Figuring out the rules," he replied. "That's what any scientist is doing. And anyone who claims otherwise is just a philosopher in disguise."

"What's the difference?"

"Science is about discovering *how* things work," Browntree explained. "Not about why."

"But isn't why the most important part?"

"'Why' is irrelevant," he said. "The earth spins on an axis. Science showed us that. We can prove it. Why does it spin on an axis? To do anything else would preclude the existence of life. Why do we need to know why? All that's important is how. Can you do anything about why? Is there a remedy for why? Of course not. Why is as it is. How is what we can see, and what we can measure."

"Why is what it means," Abigail said.

"Are you looking for a meaning to life?"

"Isn't everyone?"

"Only the desperate," he said.

"Then I must be desperate," she replied.

"Because you believe in your God?"

"You make it sound like…"

"Like what?"

"Like it's a weakness to do so."

"Isn't it?"

"Not to me," Abby said. "You're looking at faith like it's an obstacle. You don't think why is important. I don't think there's any other question to ask."

"So, why, then?" he replied. "Is there some divine plan? And what if you did discover why? Would it make any difference?"

"You're looking for the instruction manual," Abigail countered. "I'm looking for the road map."

"And neither of us are going to find what we're looking for," Browntree said. "It's not set up that way. Every answer leads to a dozen more questions. Look at those creatures, those things, Goners, you called them. They're electricity, but not entirely. And they have a consciousness. What are they? Where did they come from? And does any of it matter as they're destroying my cabin?"

"They're ghosts," Abby said. "Or at least something like that. Something happened in these mines, the miners found something, a doorway, and when they opened it, I don't know, something came out."

"That's a lot of somethings," Browntree said. "That does corroborate it, though."

"Corroborate what?"

"Well, that's why I'm here, in a manner of speaking," Browntree said.

"Because of the Goners?"

"Because of the door," he said. "I'm an electromagneticist by training. One of about three in the world, and frankly the only one of us worth his salt. I heard about Sunset Falls quite by accident. A friend in the Forest Service told me about how electronic gadgets, flashlights, radios and the like, suddenly stopped working when they came near this area. Strange lights in the night sky, bursts of energy that knocked out radio transmissions. All manner of strange things. It intrigued me, and I came only intending to stay for a long weekend, discover some electromagnetic anomaly, and be done with it."

"But you stayed."

"For over a year now, yes. My colleagues must by now think I've left the country, or died." He shook his head. "At first it was only the electromagnetic spikes. They were impressive, very powerful. I triangulated their source and that's when I discovered they came from the mines."

"How did you find the door, then?"

"I didn't, or rather, I haven't, not yet," he said. "By the time I arrived in town, the last miner was dead and the story had already become legend. Legends stem from truth, no matter how garbled they become in the retelling. The source of the electromagnetic energy was in the tunnels, and the evidence doesn't lie."

"But the Goners don't live in the tunnels."

"That's the fascinating part," he said. "The main spike of energy is in the tunnels, yes, but these things also generate their own energy, independent of the tunnels. And in another location, too, deep in the woods. Beneath some old Indian woman's cabin."

"Not beneath," Abby replied. "Trust me."

Browntree sat back in the glow of the flashlight. His eyes narrowed.

"Who are you, really?" he asked.

"You wouldn't believe me if I told you."

"Why not?"

Abby cocked an eyebrow. "Because you'd have to take it on faith."

"Don't play games."

"My name is Abigail Crosley," she said. "My mother's name was Molly Walker, although it turns out that really wasn't her last name… it was more of a disguise."

"How's that?"

"My mother's name wasn't Walker," Abby said. "That's what she was. A Walker, a sort of wandering scavenger that feeds on the energy of human beings. She fed on positive energy. Not all of them do. But she did. And she happened upon Sunset Falls, probably because it was so isolated. And although I can't imagine it now, it must have been a happy place. She wouldn't have stayed otherwise."

"Your mother?"

Abby nodded. "She fell in love with my father, and he with her. They left town, I don't know why, but it was long before the miners died and the Red Witch came."

"Witches too, huh?"

"Not really. It's just what they call her. The old Indian woman, from the cabin in the woods. She's a Walker, too, like my mother. Except she feeds on anger, and fear. Negative things."

"Positive and negative energy, witches who aren't really witches, people who wander around looking for human energy. You have a vivid imagination, my dear."

"I wish I did," Abby replied. "I'd love nothing more than to discover that all of it's one big hoax."

"You really believe this, then, don't you?"

"Belief doesn't figure into it," she said. "Remember? *Why* doesn't matter. Only *is* matters."

"Yes, but *is* actually needs to be a real thing," Browntree replied. "Not some convoluted ghost stories."

"And the Goners?" she asked. "How do you explain them?"

"Explanation isn't my job."

"So what is?" she exclaimed. "I think you're afraid. And not just a little boo-scared but full-out mess your pants terrified. You came here because you thought there was some simple, logical explanation for the lights and the electricity. There isn't, or you wouldn't still be here. You're afraid to find out what's really going on, and you're afraid to leave."

"That's preposterous."

"Is it? Then why did you build your electric pulse machine, or whatever it is? Certainly not to find out what's going on around here.

You already knew. That's why you built something to protect yourself. You know what's happening in this town isn't anything ordinary. It's extraordinary, and it's defying your ability to explain it. You're on the verge of discovering something really important, but you won't let yourself see it. It requires a leap of faith, and you won't take it."

"Because it's foolish to do so!"

"More foolish than closing your eyes?" Abby asked. "Look, you built that burst machine, and you used it to help me. That tells me you're not entirely pigheaded."

"Pigheaded?"

"Maybe you can open your eyes a little and take a look at what the evidence has already shown you," Abigail said. "You saw the Goners. You recognized the danger. You've discovered the energy of the Red Witch's cabin. It's not that big a leap to at least listen to me."

"None of it's possible."

"Of course it's not possible, it just *is*. Isn't that your whole argument? Don't worry about naming it, just recognize it? Or does that only apply to questions of religious faith?"

Browntree considered this for a long time. He ran his long fingers through his even longer hair. Abigail pulled her knees up to her chest, then, remembering she was wearing only a nightgown, brought them modestly down again.

"Why did you ask me if I believe in God?" Browntree asked.

"It was just a question."

"No, 'hot enough for you?' is just a question. You're not telling me everything, are you?"

"I don't know what you're…"

"Come on, Abigail, I think we're well past that point, don't you?"

Abby sighed, frustrated. "Yes, all right, there is more."

"I thought so."

"You don't need to be so glib about it."

Browntree shrugged. "Glib is what I do best."

"You do it well."

"I can't help you if you don't level with me."

"You're going to help me now?"

"If what you're telling me is true, then I don't think I have much choice."

"No, I suppose not."

"So?"

"My mother was a Walker."

"Yes, so you said."

"And as her daughter, I have certain… I don't know, powers, abilities," Abby said. "Not like her. I'm not a full-blood, that's what the Goners called her, a full-blood. They called me a half-blood. I'm not her, but there is something special about me. That's what the Red Witch told me."

"You've met this Red Witch, then?"

She nodded. "My uncle took me to her. I think he wanted to, I don't know, trade me to her. I'm not sure why."

"I'm still listening."

Abby continued. "The Goners said something like that, too. That I have some sort of ability. That's why they're after me, I think. There's something I'm able to do, or some connection I'm able to make that will help them."

"Which is?"

"I don't know."

"I see."

"You're a real creep, do you know that?"

"Because I'm skeptical?" Browntree asked. "Goodness, a little healthy skepticism is just what this town needs."

"But your knee-jerk skepticism isn't helping anyone."

"Okay, let's say everything you've told me is true," he replied. "Hypothetically, of course, but for the sake of argument, let's make some assumptions. Let's say your mother was a, what did you call it, a Walker? And let's say there really is a door at the end of this mineshaft that some fool miners accidentally opened and some manner of, what, evil? Malevolence? was released. And let's say these Goners are a direct result of that. And we'll further say that you, being the half-breed child of some supernatural entity and a local boy, are at the center of it. What next? What conclusions do we draw from it? Are they all after you? What for? What are these mysterious powers you've got, and why are they so desperately craved by these otherworldly entities?"

"Now you're just making fun of me."

"What do you expect?" Browntree queried. "You're asking me to believe something that I know to be factually impossible. Even if I could believe what you're telling me, and I must say, I'm beginning to believe that *you* believe it, even it I could swallow any of it down, what do you want me to do?"

"You're the only one with a weapon."

Browntree rolled his eyes. "It's not a weapon, Abigail, it's an electromagnetic disbursement device. I'm not certain it even works, despite our episode the previous night. And even if it does, is it even still in one piece? Whatever happened to my cabin looked and sounded as if it was quite thorough."

"You're here, aren't you?" she asked.

"What does that mean?"

"It means you believe that something's going on, or else you wouldn't have left your cabin and all that equipment. Look, I'm not asking you to solve my problem. I'm not even sure it is my problem. All I did was stumble across your cabin in the dark. But you're a smart man, that's obvious. Just help me think it through."

Browntree sighed. "All right. I don't like it, but all right."

"Thank you."

"These powers, abilities, whatever you say you have. What are they?"

"I don't know."

"So what makes you think that …"

"Because everyone around me seems to think I'm dangerous. It's making me nervous."

"Do they know you don't know?"

"I'm not sure. I think they're starting to catch on. They've had to explain a lot to me, the Goners and the Red Witch. I think they believe I know more than I really do."

"Do you?"

"I just told you that…"

"Level with me or I can't help you."

"All right, yes, there's one more thing."

Browntree cocked his head. "Which is?"

"I hear things," Abby replied.

"What things?"

"Voices," she said. "Or I think they're voices. I started hearing them when we first got here. They were barely whispers then. I thought my brother was playing a trick on me."

"And now?"

"They're louder," she replied. "Much louder. Distinct, too. Like snatches of a hundred different conversations, all tumbling over each other."

"Do you recognize the voices?"

"No, none of them are familiar."

"Are they talking to you?"

Abby shook her head. "It's like our telephone line back in the city. They called it a party line."

"Yes, I had one, too," Browntree replied. "When you share a telephone line with multiple people, and sometimes you pick up the phone and there's already a conversation going on."

"Exactly, except this is like a lot of conversations going on, and none of them seem aware of the others. I just hope I'm not going crazy."

"You're quite lucid," Browntree said. "In fact, you appear to be one of the most coherent people I've ever spoken with."

"Thank you."

"But that doesn't dismiss the voices," he said. "If we rule out insanity, all we're left with is that they're real and you're really hearing them."

"What are they, then?"

Browntree furrowed his brow. "Since we're playing this little 'belief in the face of reason' game, let's make some suppositions."

"Fine."

"First, these voices you're hearing have gotten stronger, correct?"

"Yes."

"So we can infer that whatever is causing you to hear these voices is getting stronger. But what is it that's getting stronger?"

"They sound like they're getting closer."

"Closer?"

"Yes."

Browntree scratched his chin. "Closer. That's an interesting thing to say."

"Why? Now there's something you're not telling me."

"Perhaps."

"What?"

"My instruments have been recording an increase in electromagnetic discharge."

"What does that mean?" Abby asked.

"It means that maybe what you're telling me isn't so far-fetched, after all."

"Then you do believe me."

Browntree lowered his eyes. "I'm beginning to think that whatever is happening, whatever the explanation, it is increasing. Precisely what that means, and how it will play out, I can't guess."

Abby smiled for the first time since she'd met Huckleberry

Browntree. Her expression was so authentic, and her smile so pretty, that he couldn't help but smile himself.

"I don't disbelieve you, you know," he said. "I don't want to believe you, but you have made it hard to do otherwise."

"I think I might be able to sleep now," she said. "If that's okay with you."

"Of course," Browntree replied. "I'll stay up. Stand guard, as it were."

"Stand guard against what?"

Browntree smiled a small, shrewd smile. "If what you're saying is true, it could be just about anything."

Chapter Fourteen
Partial Credit

Ben woke with a start. Sunlight filled the mouth of the mineshaft. He thought he'd gone in farther than he did, but it appeared he'd only made it a dozen feet. Far enough, apparently, because he was still in one piece, but…

The Goners were gone. Were goners, he thought, and laughed. Except it wasn't a happy laugh. It was the sort of laugh that led you down to dark places. All alone.

The air from the mine was cool. He felt it almost like a breeze against his back. It wasn't a breeze, though. It was solid. Like it was breathing.

No, stupid, don't think like that. Those kinds of thoughts were bad, very bad. Like laughing. Like eyes in the dark.

Voices. At first behind him (behind him!) then outside, in the forest, and carried by the echo into the tunnel. Mens' voices, gruff and heavy. Ben crawled toward the edge of the shaft. He was careful to stay in the shadows. They weren't safe voices. He wasn't being rescued. The voices didn't know he was there. Shadows were his ally, and he used them.

For a moment, he didn't see anything. The forest was thick, and closer to the mineshaft than it had seemed the night before. Everything was different in the light of day.

A man appeared. He was tall, with a round, jowled face. Another man followed close behind, shorter, dressed in black, and another, stooped over as he walked. Trailing behind was his Uncle Dutch. Ben huddled as far back in the tunnel as he could.

"…utterly out of control," the man dressed in black was saying. He spoke loudly, and Ben guessed he was the town's reverend.

"That's why we gotta' do this," Dutch replied. "C'mon, Re'v'rnd, we been through this enough times t'know we got no more choices."

"We boxed ourselves into a corner," the tall man's jowls shook as he spoke. "This is our own doin'. The Red Witch came 'cause we was arrogant. We thought we'd never have no more troubles. If it weren't for that girl - -"

"Leave Molly out of it," Dutch growled.

"Can't do that, Dutch," the stooped man said. "Everything that's happenin' now started back then with her."

"Let's just deal with the problem now," Dutch said.

Reverend Martin shook his head. "We all know what she means

to ya', Dutch. We all loved her. But it don't change what she was, or what she did."

"All she did was leave," Dutch replied.

The jowly man shrugged. "Seems that was everything."

The men crossed to the other side of the clearing and headed back into the woods. From his vantage point in the mine, Ben struggled to listen. He was intrigued now. They were talking about his mother. He looked around quickly, believing that at any moment the Goners would leap out to finish what they'd started the previous night. No one was there, and the weird electric tingling he'd experienced when they were close by wasn't there, either. Ben took a breath, summoned his courage and followed the men into the forest.

They weren't far ahead, and spoke loud enough for him to hear them clearly without having to be seen. Ben stayed low and stepped from shadow to shadow. At one point Dutch, at the end of their line, looked back sharply as if he'd heard something. Otherwise, Ben followed undetected.

The four men stepped into another clearing. Beyond them, bathed in morning sunlight, was a cabin. Yet even in such beautiful surroundings, leaves blowing in a soft breeze, dappled sunlight on weathered shingles, the place looked… dangerous, that was the only word Ben could come up with, and it only partially described the feeling he got while staring at it. There was also sadness, and grief, and, strangest of all, a sense of homecoming, although he knew he'd never seen this place before. Ben hugged the rough bark of an enormous oak tree and tried to sort out his myriad feelings.

"What are we gonna' say to her?" Reverend Martin asked, and laughed uncomfortably. "I think I'm speechless for the first time in my life."

"We'll ask her t'be fair," the jowled man replied. "She ain't been unreasonable so far."

"What rock have *you* been hidin' under, Dick Maloney?" Dutch asked. "Don't your general store have windows?"

"Knock it off, Dutch," the jowly Maloney said. "All I meant was - -"

"We know what you meant," the stooped man replied. "An' maybe it's time we made ourselves some tough decisions."

"Like what?" the Reverend asked.

"Like what we're prepared t'do t'get our town back," the stooped man said. "What we're willin' t'sacrifice."

"Ain't we sacrificed enough already?" Dutch asked.

"Your sacrifice has only begun," a voice called, and all four men, as well as Ben, turned to face the cabin.

At first, Ben wanted to laugh. He almost did, too, and then thought better of it. The Red Witch who stood on her rickety front porch was nearly as wide as she was tall. He single long braid of hair hung over her left shoulder. She wore a brown dress that might have at one time been a grain sack. Her feet were bare and filthy. Taken at face value, she looked about as dangerous as mashed potatoes. And yet, Ben knew what she was. Even as he sniggered at her humble appearance, a part of him, a very deep and troubled part of him, saw her for what she was. Dangerous had been an accurate description when he'd first seen the cabin. This tiny woman was a predator, not a scavenger. Maybe she had been a scavenger once, but that had changed. Ben felt the change in her, almost smelled it on her. Her evolution had happened quickly, and she had the hunger of the newly converted.

"You've brought your friends this time, Dutch Crosley," the Red Witch said. "Too afraid to come closer?"

"We want to talk," Dutch said.

The Witch smiled. "You want to negotiate."

Dutch was about to answer when Reverend Martin stepped forward.

"Red Witch, I'm Reverend Martin, from the town," he said sweetly, as if addressing the Church Ladies Auxiliary instead of evil itself.

"You've brought me your holy man?" the Red Witch asked. Her dark eyes sparkled with either mirth or outrage, Ben couldn't be sure.

"Red Witch, now, the four of us have come here on behalf of the whole town," Reverend Martin continued. "To ask you, no, *implore* you, to appeal to your good nature and free us all from this… unpleasantness that's been goin' on."

The Red Witch regarded him. "And what unpleasantness would that be?"

Reverend Martin cleared his throat. "To be quite truthful, and meaning no disrespect, of course, the unpleasantness that you yourself have caused."

"I see," the Red Witch said. She looked at each man in turn, and then into the woods and, Ben felt, directly at him.

"It pains me to hear you speak such things, Reverend," the Witch replied. "I believe I've made it perfectly clear at whose feet the blame should lie. Didn't we discuss this at great length already, Dutch Crosley? No, the blame for your town's decline is not mine. The blame lies with you, each of you, and every one of your cowering, frivolous townspeople. Your fear has called your troubles to you. I didn't bring it."

"But you can stop it," the stooped man said.

A wide grin spread across the Red Witch's face.

"For a price," she said.

"What is it you want?" Reverend Martin asked.

"You know what I want!" the Red Witch's voice thundered through the clearing.

"But she's gone," Dutch said.

"She isn't far," the Red Witch said. "Closer than you think. The Walker's daughter hides in the abandoned mines."

"If you know where she is, why don't you just - -?"

"Because it's beyond my influence," the Witch hissed. "There are rules for this, even for me. I had her once."

"But she got away," Dutch said.

"I underestimated her then," the Witch replied. "But not again. Bring me the girl and your town will be spared."

Dick Maloney cleared his throat and stepped forward.

"You told us that once before," he said, his voice trembling. "And we gave you a sacrifice, and yet you're still here."

The Witch was quiet for a long time. When she spoke again, her voice was low and seemed to hover over the clearing like a fog.

"You try my patience," she said. "I have done all I can for you. You're under the mistaken impression that what has happened to your town is the worst that will happen, and that I am in some way responsible for escalating it. In fact, I have upheld my end of our original bargain by providing what protection I can to all of you. You think those ridiculous Goners are the worst that's out there? They're inconsequential, that's why I've allowed them to remain. If not for my protection, the door that your foolish men so recklessly opened would have welcomed in such a host of unsavory things that you would be begging for a Goner or two by now."

"But if you can keep those things at bay, can't you also seal the door forever?" Reverend Martin asked.

The Witch considered this.

"It is possible," she said.

"Then what do we need to do to - -?"

"You know what I want."

The men looked at each other, uncomfortable at being backed into a corner.

"Don't look like we got much choice," Dick Maloney said.

"We gotta' go find your niece, Dutch," the stooped man agreed.

"No," Dutch said. "We ain't gonna' do this. Not this time. We've heard your promises time an' again, an' every time it's been a lie."

"Stop it, Dutch!" Reverend Martin said. "We ain't here t'make things worse. We gotta' do whatever we can."

The Reverend turned to the Witch.

"You seem a reasonable sort," he said. "An' while it's true the Walker girl ain't here now, Dutch did, in fact, already bring her to you. The way I figure, an' forgive me if I'm talkin' out of turn, but don't that at least give us partial credit?"

The Red Witch cocked her head. From his vantage point, Ben couldn't tell whether she was amused or outraged. A bit of both, as it turned out.

"Partial credit?" the Witch asked. "Well, yes, I suppose fair is fair, isn't it? You may have partial credit, then."

The Reverend sighed and seemed quite relieved.

"What does partial credit get us?" the stooped man asked.

The Witch smiled. "I'll only remove part of my protection."

And then as if a switch had been turned on, the ground began to rumble. The air crackled with electric energy. And in the woods all around Ben, things started to move.

"What's going on?" Reverend Martin shouted.

The Red Witch didn't answer, and instead turned and stepped back into her cabin.

The rumbling became a tremor, and the tremor became a shake. It felt like an earthquake, or a long explosion. The air was thick with static electricity. The hair on Ben's neck stood up. His skin twitched.

"We gotta' get home!" Dick Maloney yelled. The other men didn't wait to debate it. They took off running through the woods.

Ben followed close behind them. He didn't care now if he was seen. The men didn't look back. The five of them ran hard through the woods. All around them, energy seemed to be collecting. Ben couldn't see what it was becoming—only that it was becoming something. He caught only glimpses out of the corners of his eyes, snapshots of terrifying things, ghostly shapes and impossibly awful faces. But he was running too fast to see things clearly. He was thankful for that. He thought if he actually saw what was forming in the woods, if he actually looked at any of it head-on, he'd probably go insane.

They passed the clearing where Ben had first seen his uncle and the other men. The mineshaft loomed dark and ominous. Yet in comparison to the growing terror in the woods, the mine was the lesser evil.

Abigail was in the mine, that's what the Red Witch had said. Safe for the moment, yes, but for how long? Would the terrible energy the Witch had unleashed be bound by the same rules as she? Would its influence end at the entrance to the mine, or reach into the tunnels themselves? Ben knew he had to find his sister, and soon. She was at the center of the whole thing. He didn't know how, or why, or even what she could do to stop it, but Ben was certain that Abigail could do something.

The four men fled through the woods toward town, but Ben cut through the clearing and ran back into the dark sanctuary of the mine.

Chapter Fifteen

Sounds & Visions

Abigail awoke with a thick hand covering her mouth. She fought against it, but Huckleberry Browntree shushed her.

"We're not alone," he said, and took his hand away.

It occurred then to Abby that the lamps were out. The mine was dark, and very cold. The darkness seemed to amplify the chill. Abby remembered she was still only in her nightgown, and shivered.

And yes, they were not alone.

It sounded at first like mice scuffling in the dark. Abby thought the darkness was magnifying the sound, the same as it was with the cold, but then she heard a thud and knew it was very close.

Huck leaned close to her ear. His breath smelled stale, and with a hint of cloves.

"If it can't see us, it can't find us," he said.

"Are you so sure?" she whispered.

"Listen to it stumbling around. It's as blind as we are."

And sure enough, whatever it was stumbled over something metallic and caused a terrible, echoing ruckus. It was closer now, perhaps in the main tunnel right outside their alcove. Abby reached around on the floor.

"What are you doing?" Huck asked. "Sit still."

"If it was gonna' get us, it would've gotten us already," she said. "Where's the flashlight?"

"Are you crazy?"

"Not yet," she replied. "But if I keep sitting around in the dark trying to figure out what those sounds are, I just might consider it."

Her hand found the metal handle of Browntree's flashlight. She picked it up and aimed it in the direction of the sounds.

"What are you - -?" Huck began, but Abigail had already turned the light on.

For a moment, everything stopped. The light shocked them all, Abby and Browntree and even Ben, who was caught in its glow. It took Abby a full dozen seconds to recognize her brother. Then she screamed. Ben screamed, too, followed by Huck. Abby dropped the light and ran to her brother.

They held onto each other for a long time. For both of them, it was like a happy ending to a bad dream. The fact that Abby had left him alone, the reality of their terrible situation, all of it was forgotten and they were just family again.

After several long moments of this, Huck picked up the flashlight and cleared his throat. He pointed the light at the siblings and they reluctantly parted.

"It's my brother," Abby said. "Ben, this is Huckleberry Browntree."

Ben raised his eyebrows. "Your name's really - -?"

"Yes, it's a family name."

"Okay."

"Mr. Browntree kind of saved me from the Goners," Abby said.

"Kind of?" Huck scoffed.

"All right, *did*," she replied, then turned her attention back to Ben. "You look awful. What happened to you?"

"This morning or last night?"

"It's morning already?" Huck asked. "Can't tell in here."

"Start at the beginning, Ben, and then I'll go," Abby said. She led her brother into the small alcove that had been hers' and Huck's refuge.

They re-lit the oil lamps and Ben recounted his plight. He started with Dutch and Penny, her awful words to him, then finding Gus and being nearly annihilated by the rest of the Goners. He finished with the morning's events, the men from the town and the Red Witch. Abby whistled through her teeth when he finished, and shook her head.

"Then it's worse than I thought," she said. "The things in the woods. Did you get a good look at them?"

Ben shook his head. "I can't remember them enough to explain them, but I know I'll never forget them."

"How do you mean?" Browntree asked.

Ben furrowed his brow. "It's like they didn't want to be seen, or maybe they couldn't really *be* seen. They were there, I know that much. But it was almost like I was just *feeling* them, not actually seeing them."

"Explain that," Huck said.

Ben glanced at his sister. "Who *is* this guy?"

Abby laughed a little. "He's okay, don't worry. He's a scientist. He asks a lot of questions."

"He's sitting right here, if you don't mind," Huck said. "Please, Ben, is it?"

"Yeah."

"You said the Red Witch told the men from town that their fear had caused this. Is that what you felt? Fear?"

"Yeah, sure, of course. It was terrifying."

"But those things in the woods didn't seem real?"

"What are you getting at?" Abby asked.

"Nothing yet, but something's forming," Huck replied. "Ben, was it like they didn't have a form?"

Ben shook his head. "I saw things, real things, y'know, like they were there. Only, I've never really felt that way before. If I see something, like I'm looking across at you now, I don't feel like you're not there. The things I saw in the woods, the things I glimpsed, well, it felt like I wasn't really seeing them."

Huck sat back against the wall, tugging at his unshaven chin. "I see," he said.

"You see what?" Abigail asked. "Come on, if you know something, let us know."

"It's nothing concrete," he replied. "Just part of a hypothesis I've been working out since I first encountered those things, those Goners. They're mostly electricity, you know."

"Yeah, I felt that, too," Ben said. "When I was with them last night, it was like an electrical storm off in the distance, but getting closer."

"But what does that have to do with --?" Abigail began, but Huck held up a silencing hand. For a moment they heard nothing, and Abby was about to lay into him for frightening her again, when a sound echoed down the passageway.

"What was that?" Ben asked.

"That wasn't you?" Abby replied.

"I'm sitting right here."

"That came from down the tunnel," Huck said.

"Which direction?" Abby asked. "The entrance?"

Huck shook his head. "I don't think so."

He stood up quickly, nearly knocking over one of the lamps.

"We've got to get moving," he said. "And fast."

"Should we blow out the lanterns?" Abby asked.

"We're going to need them," Huck said. "We've got to get out of these tunnels."

They stood up fast, grabbing the bags and lanterns, and stepped into the main tunnel.

"Do you feel that in the air?" Huck asked.

"It tingles, yeah," Abby replied. "It's like an electrical charge, like before a storm."

"They're down here," Huck said.

"The Goners can't come down here," Ben argued. "Gus said so. That's why they couldn't - -"

"I don't think those are the Goners," Huck replied. "Run!"

They followed his bobbing flashlight as he led them through the tunnel. Wooden beams on the walls and over their heads resembled ribs in some giant gutted animal. Rail tracks ran through the middle of the floor. Their metal reflected the flashlight beam.

Something heavy hit the wall behind them. Ben yelped.

"Keep running!" Browntree called.

"What is it?" Abby asked.

"Keep running!" Browntree repeated.

Abby slowed down and peered into the gloom behind them. Ben crashed into her and the two nearly fell.

"Move!" Ben shouted.

"But what *is* it?" Abby asked.

"Who cares?" Huck replied. "It's getting closer!"

A Y-junction in the passageway loomed ahead.

"Which way?" Huck asked.

"I don't remember," Abby replied.

"Right!" Ben called. "Take the right!"

Whatever it was behind them made a slithering, gelatinous sound, punctuated by a sharp metallic clink that could have been anything, but sounded for all the world like large, heavy scales scraping against the rail tracks. Ben could see it in his mind… a great slithering beast with armor-like scales covering its belly, sliding through the narrow mineshaft with easy familiarity. He pictured its teeth (of course it had massive teeth), and its yellow eyes. Ben ran harder, practically riding on his sister's back.

The right tunnel narrowed, and split off again. This time there were no more rail tracks.

"Wrong way!" Huck called. "Now what?"

"There, up ahead," Abby shouted. "I see light!"

And sure enough, and even despite the glow of Browntree's flashlight, blue-white light pierced the gloom not far down the left tunnel. They ran as fast as they could along the rocky ground. Their footsteps echoed. For a moment, Ben couldn't hear the slithering beast behind them. Then it was there again, louder, closer.

"A ladder!" Huck called. "Must be an access shaft. Follow me!"

Browntree leaped onto the metal ladder, his long hair flying like smoke from his head. His body clanged as he hit the ladder, but if it hurt he didn't show it. He was climbing without missing a step, and Abby was right behind him.

The ladder led up a thin, round tunnel running straight up over their heads. The light they'd seen came from daylight pouring in through a grate high above them. Huck climbed as fast as he could, and was nearly halfway up before Ben got to the ladder.

It was right behind him. If Ben had stopped or faltered at all, he could have seen the great horrible jaws and been snagged by one of the massive tentacles. He followed close behind his sister. Abby's nightgown fluttered in his eyes and blinded him. But he was following her up and that was all he needed to see.

He was six feet from the top when it grabbed him. Huck had the grate open and was crawling out. Abby was nearly there, and Ben was beginning to imagine that even he was going to make it out.

A thick tentacle grabbed his leg. Enormous suckers cut through his pajama pants and into his bare leg. The pain was awful. He cried out. Pain and shock nearly cost him his balance. But he held on to the ladder, tugging hard against the horrible thing that had him trapped.

Another tentacle shot out of the darkness and grabbed his other leg. Ben thought it might be a blessing that he couldn't actually see what was happening. Maybe it made it worse. Not knowing made everything worse, and bigger, and meaner, and harder to handle.

"The flashlight!" he yelled. "Quick!"

Abby had climbed out and was now climbing back down. Browntree handed her the flashlight, and she passed it to her brother. Ben took it and shone it down at his tangled legs.

There was nothing there.

At first he didn't believe it, the pain in his legs was too awful, how could there not be - - then he realized there was no pain in his legs. It wasn't like it was there and just went away with time, like a cramp… it just wasn't there anymore. He raised the flashlight and shone it in Abby face. He was about to tell her the good news when it grabbed him again. This time it was harder, and it nearly pulled him down. He shone the flashlight down again, certain that this time there had to be - -

Nothing. It was like whatever was down there didn't exist, at least not in the light. Ben concentrated the beam down to the bottom of the shaft, but all he could see was rock and the bottom rungs of the ladder.

"Where is it, Ben?" Abby cried. "Has it got you? What is it?"

"It's not there," Ben said. "I don't know how, but it's just not there anymore."

"Get him up here," Huck called. Abby pulled her brother up over her own body and through the mouth of the tunnel. Ben kept the light pointed down the whole time.

Above ground, in the light of day, his terror at what turned out to be nothing seemed childish. But he knew what he'd felt, and as he helped Browntree pull Abby out of the shaft, Ben was sure he heard a thick, wet slither.

Chapter Sixteen

Fear Itself

They all slept, including Huck. When they awoke, the sun was setting over an expanse of far-off hills. Their own shadows were getting long. They stood beside the mine's access vent (now safely closed), and stared into the distance.

"Potters Ridge," Browntree said. "The top of the hill. We can't get any higher and still be in Sunset Falls."

"What do we do now?" Ben asked.

"What do you mean?" Abby replied.

"I mean, do we go back down?"

Abby furrowed her brow. "Of course we go back. Why wouldn't we go - -?"

"Because we've got a way out now," Ben said.

Neither Abby nor Huck answered him. They looked out over the Appalachian horizon, then down into the dark valley below.

"We've got a choice here," Ben continued. "Their problems aren't our problems. We can leave right now and let this horrible little place get what it deserves."

"I'm not sure any place deserves to get wiped out," Abby replied. "No matter how bad they've been."

"Ben's right on one count," Huck said. "We do have a choice. Well, more of a choice than we did a day ago."

"To leave?" Abby asked.

"Or stay," Huck replied. "Because staying is now a choice. If we recognize that, we see all our choices with open eyes."

"We *have* no choices here," Abby said. "At least I don't. I hadn't felt it before now, at least not in a way I could put into words, but I'm stuck. I'm connected to Sunset Falls in a way I don't really understand. I'm meant to do something. I don't know what, and I don't know how, but there's a reason I'm here."

"C'mon, Abby, we got dropped here," Ben argued. "That's it. There's no big meaning. And *that* way," he pointed to the crimson, sunset hills beyond, "is our way out."

"Then go," Abby replied. "You and Huck, start walking and don't look back."

"I'm not going without you," Ben said.

"And I'm not going," Abby fumed.

"Whatever we do," Browntree interjected, "we need to do it together. Ben, I agree with your sister. I'm a man of science, of reason… I don't accept signs, I never have. But I also don't accept blind fear, either. Running away… it's not reasonable."

"Reasonable?" Ben asked. "I think we're a long way past reasonable. Whatever's going on in that valley, it sure as heck isn't reasonable. Why are you continuing to look at it like some science experiment, with some rational explanation that you can measure and put down in a notebook? It's beyond reasonable. It's beyond rational. I think running away is the most reasonable thing we can do."

"If we do that, we give in to the only weapon this phenomenon has," Huck replied.

"Which is?"

"Fear," Huck said, and ran a hand through his unruly hair. "I'm as guilty of irrationality as anyone. Maybe not to the extent of the town elders, but nearly so. My instinct, when faced with all I've seen, has been to run scared. First from the Goners, then from whatever was in that mine shaft."

"That was a good instinct," Ben quipped.

"And it was the wrong instinct," Huck replied.

"You know something, don't you?" Abby asked.

Browntree shrugged sheepishly. "Not with any certainty, but - -"

"Tell us."

He sighed. "It was more or less a hunch until the mine shaft," he said. "We were all certain we were being chased, so certain that our bodies reacted as if we were."

"Because we *were* being chased," Ben replied. "I heard it. I *felt* it."

"But when you turned the flashlight on it, whatever it was wasn't there. How could that be?"

Ben shook his head. "It let go quickly, it was afraid of the light, I don't know."

"I'm beginning to believe it wasn't even there to begin with."

"But I felt it," Ben argued. "It grabbed me."

"Where's the evidence of it?" Huck asked. "You said it grabbed your leg, you felt it through your pajama leg. And yet your leg has no marks. Your pajamas are intact. Nothing is ripped, your leg isn't even bruised. And we never saw the creature."

"You're saying that thing was never even there?" Ben asked.

"No, not exactly," Huck replied. "I'm saying it was there because we brought it there. Was it empirically real? No. Was it real to us? Yes, completely so."

"What about the Goners?" Abigail asked. "Are they figments of our imaginations, too? Because they sure seemed real enough to me."

"Me, too," Ben added.

"I'm not talking about imagination," Browntree explained. "Or even some sort of group hypnosis, which I had considered. No, there is something real at the heart of it all. I'm talking about our *reactions* to it. And not just us, the entire town. If we accept that your mother was what everyone claims she was, a sort of emotional parasite, excuse my crude analogy, or scavenger of feelings, and then it is possible she left Sunset Falls because there was no more positive energy. Something dark and sad took over. That's what drew the Red Witch, and that's what hangs over this town today."

"But what is it?" Abby asked. "If it's real, then what is it?"

"I'm not even sure that matters," Huck replied. "Whatever sadness or darkness caused it, events are far beyond it now. Fear is like a brush fire, it just needs a single spark to light it and it's out of control before anyone realizes it. Fear is the problem now, and whatever must be done, whatever purpose Abigail has here, it's the symptom that must be treated. I've never seen more fear than I've seen here. Irrational fear, blind fear. We felt it in the tunnels, and with the Goners, too. And Ben in the forest, and at almost every other turn. I don't believe it matters anymore what set this fire. It's out of control, and it will burn us all to the ground."

"Unless we stop it," Abigail replied.

"I don't know that that's even possible anymore," Huck said. "On one level, the town wants to be free, but on another it's become a sort of badge of honor. Their identity as a town, and as individuals in it, is tied up with their fear. They've been at it so long, and wallowing in it so long, that it's become almost pleasurable. They don't *remember* anything else. Their daily routine, from never going out when it's dark to their uneasy truce with the Red Witch, it's all they know. They're so fiercely proud of their isolation, and so afraid of losing what makes them unique, that they've embraced this fear-life as their reality. That's why I say it's not imagination. Imagination can't be measured, and I've measured the energy here. The Goners are the manifestation of that energy now, but recent events lead me to believe that darker things have begun to emerge. Your experience in the woods, Ben, when you ran from the Witch's cabin… you didn't see it clearly, but you got a sense that something terrible was out there. The town's fear is growing, and the manifestations of that fear are growing, as well."

"So it's all make-believe, then?" Ben asked.

Browntree shook his head. "Not in the least. Fear is a powerful emotion. Amplified by whatever dark energy is at its heart, this fear is a living, breathing thing. It's tangible. *Measurable.* I've measured it. So in a sense, it's real. As real as anything else."

"But it's only just a feeling," Abigail said.

Huck shook his head again. "Any reality is just an interpretation. My reality is only my view of things. So is yours, and Ben's, and your aunt and uncle's, and the town's. What we see and smell and touch, we process through our minds. Our processing is imperfect. We filter everything through a sieve that colors our reality with our own particular and peculiar views. Reality is a matter of interpretation. Your reality isn't my reality. Everything we see and experience is tainted by our histories and associations and prejudices and yes, our fears. Especially our fears. Empirical reality just doesn't exist, at least not from the perspective of the human mind. Maybe there is one central reality, but it doesn't much matter to us. We can't see it, anyway."

"I don't buy it," Ben said.

Huck was exasperated. "There's nothing for sale," he replied. "It's not a matter of belief. We'll leave matters of faith to Reverend Martin. This is simply the nature of the human mind."

"But how can we all agree on what we've seen?" Ben asked. "I mean, we've all seen the Goners. We all heard what was in the tunnels."

"How do you know that what I heard was what you heard?" Browntree replied. "How do you know that my interpretation is the same as your interpretation? Or your sisters'? What you see when you look at the Goners and what I see are different. We're interpreting the same stimuli but coming to our own separate conclusions."

"But then, doesn't that make the Goners real?" Ben asked. "If all we're doing is interpreting them?"

"In a sense, yes."

"This is silly," Ben said.

Huck pursed his lips. "Is love real?"

"Love's an emotion," Ben replied.

"Do you feel it?"

"Yeah, sure."

Browntree shrugged. "Is it real?"

Ben thought about this. "Not like you are, or Abby is. I can reach out and touch both of you."

"You love your sister."

"Of course."

"But if love doesn't really exist, how can you feel it?"

"It's different," Ben said.

"How is it different?"

"It's a feeling, not something real."

"But you say you love your sister," Browntree said.

"Not in a way I can reach out and touch."

"How do you know you love your sister?"

Ben narrowed his eyes. "Because I can feel it."

"Feelings *are* real, not necessarily because we can reach out and touch them, but because we act upon them. They're stimuli, they're… they're measurable because we react to them. They are a cause to an effect. Love, hate, fear, all of it is part of an unseen thread that winds through our lives. We react to how we feel. Feelings may not be visible, but they're most certainly real."

"And I'm getting a very real sense that we've got to find some place to spend the night," Abigail said. "The valley's already dark, and, fear or not, I'm not interested in being caught outside tonight."

"So what do we do now?" Ben asked.

"I'm not leaving," Abby said. "Not yet, not 'til I find out what's going on."

"And I'm not leaving you," Ben replied.

"So it looks like we're going back down there," Browntree said, and shrugged. "Ah, well, I suppose in for a penny, in for a pound."

"What does that mean?" Ben asked.

"It means, if we're going to do it, let's do it," Huck replied.

Abby peered into the gloom of the forest below them. From their vantage point, they could see most of the valley. Dutch and Penny's house was far off to the left, and the town itself farther still. The steeple of Reverend Martin's small church caught the last of the day's fading light.

"Look, down there," Abby pointed to a spot nearly straight down the hillside.

"What is it?" Ben asked.

"It's a cabin," Abby said. "It's small, but there are no lights on. Maybe no one's home."

Ben was about to speak when there came an enormous rumble from the valley below. Something heavy was moving, rustling the treetops and advancing quickly.

"Whether or not it's vacant, I don't think we have much choice," Browntree said.

"Bring the lanterns," Abigail ordered. "I want as much light as we can get tonight."

The three companions, sister and brother and electromagnetician, climbed as quickly as they dared down the steep hillside toward the safety of the dark cabin.

Chapter Seventeen

Talks by the Fire

The cabin was, in fact deserted, although not devoid of comforts. A table and chairs sat near an empty kitchen, while two rocking chairs faced a large stone fireplace. Two small bedrooms were off the main room. Browntree lit a fire and soon sooty warmth replaced the damp chill. The cabin had once been someone's home, but had been abandoned in a hurry… so much of a hurry, in fact, that both Ben and Abigail were able to find clothes to wear.

The firelight cast a comforting glow over the cabin. Huck sat at the table and wrote furiously in a notebook he pulled from his knapsack. Ben and Abby sat in the rocking chairs, drawing all the warmth they could from the fire.

"Why did you leave?" Ben asked. "I mean, without telling me?"

"I thought you were safer with Dutch and Penny," Abby replied.

Ben rocked in silence for a time, considering her words.

"I was afraid, you know."

"You're always afraid."

"I thought you were gone for good," Ben said.

"I would've come back."

"Where were you going?"

Abby glanced at him, then back at the fire.

"Away," she said. "To get help, I guess."

"You guess?"

"I don't know why I left, okay?" she exclaimed. "I was afraid, too. I was angry. We were abandoned here, and, I don't know, I just wanted out."

Ben rocked quietly. "You could've taken me."

Abigail lowered her eyes. "I know."

"Why didn't you?"

"God, Ben, quit clinging!" Abby said. "I'm not Mom, okay? Ever since she died it's been like this."

"Like what?"

"Like I can't be out of your sight," she replied. "You're thirteen, Ben, but sometimes I think you're still in diapers. I can't be your parent. I'm not Mom. Don't you think I miss her, too? I can't be that person to you because I don't know how to do it. I don't *want* to do it. I'm sixteen, it's too much. I don't have a mom, either, but I don't have anyone to lean on. It's hard enough just taking care of me. I can't take care of you."

"When Dad comes to get us…"

"Dad's not coming to get us!" Abby snapped. "Don't you realize that yet? He gave up on us, and he left us here because it was easier for him. He's never coming back."

"Yes, he is!"

"No, he isn't!" Abby argued. "Geez, Benny, you really don't get it, do you? We're in this by ourselves. No Mom, no Dad. Uncle Dutch and Aunt Penny are too consumed with themselves to take care of us. You're on your own, and so am I. That's just the way it's got to be."

Ben's eyes filled with tears, but he choked them back. He wouldn't give her the satisfaction of being weak.

"We're a family, Abigail," he said. "Like it or not. We're all we've got now."

"What family?" she asked. "One where our mother was some sort of monster, and our dad ran out on us? Mom was a freak, Ben, and thanks to her, so am I. I'm not back in this awful little valley out of any sense of family obligation. I'm here for me. I need to know who I am… I need to know *what* I am."

"Whatever you are, I'm that, too," Ben said.

"It's just the women, Benji," Abby replied. "We're the Walkers, not you. You're normal. I'm not. And if what I am is tied up in this town and their silly, stupid fears, then I've got to find it."

She stood up suddenly, shaking her furious red hair.

"I'm not your guardian angel," she said. "And I can't watch out for you anymore. I won't do it. It's just too damned hard."

Abigail walked away. Her red hair trailed behind her like volcanic fire. She went into the farthest bedroom and slammed the door. Ben stared at the closed door for a long time, then set his gaze on the fire.

"You mustn't blame her," Browntree said.

"Mustn't I?" Ben replied, sarcasm dripping like venom.

"She doesn't know who she is anymore," Huck continued. "Her world has crumbled. Her identity is gone. Who she is, even *what* she is, is a mystery to her."

"She's my sister."

"And she'll remember that, in time," Huck said. "But for now she's a mess of anger and confusion. She's lashing out at you because you *are* here. No one else is. You're getting everyone's anger."

"I don't want it."

"And she doesn't want it, either. Remember that. She's got a terrible burden at her feet. No one's even sure what that burden is, least of all her. She can't fight it if she doesn't know what it is. So she's fighting you. In a way, it's kind of a compliment."

"How's that?"

"She's pushing you away because she knows you'll always come back," he replied. "She's confident in you. She's confident in your loyalty to her."

"Like a puppy," Ben scoffed.

"Like someone who loves her," Huck said. "Look, she has to push back. When you're sixteen, everything is about reacting. What's happened to both of you has also happened to her. Do you follow me?"

"Not really."

"What you two have gone through together, losing your mom, being dropped here by your dad, finding out that your mother wasn't what you thought she was… Abigail felt it in a different way than you did. You cling to her. She's pushing away. Your sister's just dealing with it the only way she can."

"What can I do?" Ben asked.

"To stop it? Nothing, I'm afraid. Dealing with pain is a personal thing. Until she's all right with it, she'll continue to push you away. Just be there for her. Be what she pushes against."

"What if she pushes too hard?"

Browntree smiled. "Don't let her go."

They rocked together in silence for a time. Huck stoked the fire, which was dwindling. A fresh gasp of heat filled the room.

"You're smart about a lot of stuff," Ben said. Huck glanced up quickly, and then looked away.

"Smart, yes," he replied. "Involved? No."

"What do you - -?"

"I'm a good observer," Huck explained. "A keen observer, I guess you'd say. I see the patterns and the underlying meanings in things. It's clear to me, the way painting is clear to an artist, or music to a musician. That's why I'm a scientist. It's how I think. But put me in a relationship of my own? It's like I'm suddenly back in grammar school. I don't know anything anymore. I can't see the context."

"Is that why you're here?" Ben asked.

"I suppose it is, in a way," Huck replied. "It's why I'm here alone. And it's why, when and if this is ever over, I'll be returning to my little house near the university back in Charleston and live there by myself."

"No family?"

Huck shook his head. "Both parents deceased. An only child. I suppose I came by solitude naturally."

"I can't imagine being all alone."

"It's not so bad," Browntree replied. "It's an acquired taste, I think. Like broccoli."

"Yuck."

"Well, you may find you like the taste someday. I like being by myself. I don't have to contend with someone else's whims. And I don't need to worry that I'm giving more than I'm getting."

"But no one cares about you."

Huck nodded. "That's the other side of things. I don't have the bad, but I don't have the good, either."

"Do you miss it?" Ben asked. "Having your parents care about you?"

"Sometimes," Huck replied. "I miss caring about them. I miss worrying about what will happen to them. But I know how your sister feels—sometimes it's just too much to bear."

"It's worth bearing it," Ben said.

"Perhaps," Browntree sighed, and stretched his legs. "But tomorrow when the sun comes up we have other things to bear. And I'm afraid it makes your family dynamics a bit of a back-burner issue."

"You mean, like, how we convince an entire town not to be afraid anymore?"

"I hadn't thought of it quite that way, but, yes, that's it in a nutshell."

Ben frowned. "They won't listen, you know."

"I know."

"So what'll we do?"

"Show them, I think," Browntree said. "Show them there's no reason to be afraid."

"How?"

"By standing up to all that frightens them," he replied, and shrugged. "And what frightens us, too."

Ben nodded. "That's what I thought you'd say."

"You don't agree?"

"It's not that, it's just..." Ben shrugged. "Those things, the Red

Witch, the Goners, they're real. I've spoken with one of them, even. And those other things, the worse things, well, I think they might be becoming real, too."

"Not if we don't let them."

"I don't think it's up to us," Ben said. "What did you say before, that fear was like a brush fire?"

"Right."

"Then it's already out of control, I think you said that, too. So how are we supposed to, by sheer fearlessness alone, put that fire out?"

Huck shook his shaggy head. "We don't need to put it out. The town will do that on its own, once they realize what it really is."

"Hasn't that time already passed?"

"I hope not."

"That's not very reassuring."

"My work is theoretical," Browntree replied. "I never ask for guarantees, nor do I receive them."

"But what's happening here isn't theoretical," Ben countered.

Huck smiled. "You're a smart guy, just like me. Smart enough to be giving me a run for my money."

"Mr. Browntree, I - -"

"Huck. Please."

Ben nodded. "Huck, I just think it's going to take a lot more than pointing and shaking our fingers to make all this go away."

"You're thinking of your sister."

"Yeah, I am."

"You don't know how she fits in," Browntree said. "Neither do I. Heck, neither does she. Maybe she's the wild card in all of this. From what she said about what happened in the Red Witch's cabin, with that blast of energy, I think there might be a lot more to young Abigail Crosley than meets the eye."

"I'm afraid for her," Ben said.

Huck smiled. "You're not giving her the credit she deserves. She will fight as hard as she can to do all that she can do. I believe that, and I know you believe that, too. She's a strong person, your sister is. One of the strongest I've ever met. And she'll fight tooth and nail to get to the truth. I trust her, and that's saying quite a lot, since I don't generally trust anyone but myself. She's part of all this, no doubt about it. How big or small remains to be seen."

"How will we know?" Ben asked.

"When it's time, if it's ever time, your sister, like everyone, will have her hour. Until then, well, it's time to go to bed."

"I am a little tired," Ben replied, and grinned. "Okay, I'm a *lot* tired."

"I'll sit out here," Huck said. "There's another bed in there. You climb in and I'll try to keep quiet."

Ben stood up. Weariness made him sag nearly to the floor. Before he went into the bedroom, he turned to Browntree.

"I'm glad it was you," Ben said.

"How's that?"

Ben smiled. "I don't think Abigail's is the only hour that's coming."

Chapter Eighteen
Abigail's Note

Ben stretched. He'd slept late. His body felt the kind of fatigue that comes from too much sleep, or too long without it. His head was fuzzy as he shuffled out of his bed.

The cabin was quiet. At first he assumed it was because everyone was still asleep. Then something started to gnaw at him and he stepped out into the main room.

Browntree was there, slumped awkwardly in the chair where Ben had left him. Ben smiled. Browntree's hair was bunched up to one side and looked almost like a small animal was sitting on his scalp. Ben's smile faded when he checked on Abigail.

Her room was empty. The bed she'd slept in was a mess. She'd obviously had a rough night, kicking the covers off and then the sheets, too. He hoped she'd talk to him about it. After their fight, he didn't know how things would be. She was in trouble… they both were, and without each other to count on and talk to and, heck, even cry with, they'd certainly both break. Ben felt he was nearly there already, and if he couldn't talk to his sister, well, he didn't know what he'd do. Talking things through had helped him accept the loss of their mom. Now he needed Abby more than ever.

She wasn't in the cabin. At first he tried to rationalize it—she's outside, she's gone to the bathroom, she's under the bed, who knew—but a part off him already knew. She was gone.

Ben was about to wake Browntree when he noticed something on the table. It was a piece of paper, ripped from Browntree's notebook. It was a note scrawled in Abigail's unmistakable slanted handwriting:

"Dear Ben,

This is the third time I've tried to leave you behind, and this time I mean to do it properly. Every moment I'm around you I'm putting you in danger. If anything happened to you, I couldn't live with myself. This is a horrible place to be, and a horrible way to live. Not just for us, but for everyone in this town. And I can't help believing that I am somehow making it worse.

That's why I'm going to offer myself to the Witch. It will be a fair exchange—the safety of you and this town, traded for whatever it is she wants from me.

I don't know what will happen. I'm afraid. But I love you and will have no harm come to you. Don't try to follow me. It's too dangerous now. It will be over soon.

At least I hope so."

It wasn't signed, and that made it worse. Like it really was goodbye this time. Ben screamed. It was a mixture of fury and frustration and the sound of it made Huck roll clear out of his chair. He picked himself up off the floor and ran to Ben's side.

"What in the world are you --?"

"She's gone," Ben wailed. "For real this time."

"Gone?" Browntree asked. "Where?"

"To the Red Witch," Ben replied, and shoved the note into Huck's hand. "Here, read it for yourself."

He did, his bleary eyes stumbling over a few of Abby's more liberally scribbled scrawls. He lowered the letter. His face was ashen.

"This is very bad," he said.

"I know," Ben replied. "We've got to make sure she doesn't do anything stupid. Who knows what that Witch'll do to her."

"No, that's not quite it," Browntree corrected. He shook his bushy head. "Or, not the same way you mean, at least."

"What are you talking - -?"

"It's still fuzzy," Huck interrupted, "and I don't have any conclusions, but…"

"But what?" Ben asked. "Come on, if you know something about all this, now is a pretty good time to spit it out."

Browntree looked cross. "I don't *know* anything for certain, of course, but I've a few suppositions."

"Which are?"

"It's the energy, it's always been the energy," Browntree said. "But I wasn't clear on what *kind* of energy. I've been holding that there's some sort of electromagnetic imbalance, some anomaly in this part of the earth that does something to the cerebellum and creates these tremendous visions."

"I didn't see 'visions', I saw real things. I told you that."

"I know, I know," Browntree shushed him. "And that's where my flaw was. It's a *different* energy, a *hysterical* energy that doesn't have anything to do with geography. It's isolation. It's not the earth at all, don't you see? It's the people. This *town* is the energy. Their fear is what's causing this, or at least what's giving it fuel."

"But what does that have to do with my - -?"

"Your sister? Look, if we hold that what we're seeing and experiencing are real phenomena, then your sister, by the nature of what she is, is at the apex. She knew that—that's why she left town. Or tried to."

"So she did the right thing?" Ben asked.

"No, quite the opposite, I believe," Browntree replied. He shook his head. "The energy is only the beginning… no, not that. It's the firewood that keeps the entire thing stoked, but it's not the real goal."

"What *is* the goal?"

Browntree threw up his hands. Abby's note flew out of them and fell to the floor.

"That's the whole mystery," he said. His eyes narrowed. "But we can certainly hypothesize. Whatever she can do, your sister, whatever her abilities, undiscovered though they may be, it's likely quite important to this phenomenon. Abigail said something about hearing voices. Did she mention that to you?"

"The voices, yeah," Ben replied. "I thought she was playing a joke. What are they, do you think?"

Browntree shrugged. "It's hard to tell. She said they had gotten louder as time passed. I wonder…"

"You wonder what?"

"No, silly, really. Quite preposterous, actually. Because if that was true, then - -"

There was a crash outside the cabin. Ben and Huck stood motionless.

"It could be Abigail," Browntree said.

"It could also be - -"

"What?"

"Well, you name it," Ben replied. "You didn't hear what I heard in those woods."

"It's daylight," Huck said. "I don't believe those Goners or anything else lurks about at this hour."

They glanced at each other, both too afraid to move. Then, shaking his head and snorting in disgust, Browntree stepped to the door and opened it wide.

He screamed. It was a girl's body, sprawled across the front stoop. Her head, already deathly pale, was six inches removed from her grisly neck. Ben rushed to his side and sucked in his breath.

The girl sat up. Her headless torso reached for its head and, with an expert twist of the wrist, snapped it back into place. Ben and Huck stared into the grinning face of Alice the Goner.

"You can't be out now," Ben said.

"Why not?" Alice asked.

"It's not dark."

From the woods, Baby Millie shrieked with laughter. She and the others, Leopold the German and the silent, brooding black man, Abraham, appeared out of the shadows. Their silver glow was gone in the daylight. They had also become more solid.

"Lots of things changed last night," Alice said. "And lots more will change today. Mm, mm, not confined to slinking around at night.

It just proves if you stick around long enough, things always go your way."

Baby Millie shrieked again. Her banshee cry echoed in the tiny clearing.

"So, where is she?" Alice asked.

"Who?" Ben replied.

Alice flashed a rotten grin. "Play time is over, son. We've toyed with you this long because you've had some use. Don't become useless now."

"She's not here," Ben said.

"We'll see," Alice replied, and she and the other Goners burst into the cabin.

"Don't you have to be invited in or something?" Browntree asked.

"That's vampires," Alice said.

Abraham clomped heavily toward Abigail's bedroom. They knew exactly where she'd been, Ben realized. Perhaps they could smell her. More likely they just sensed her. If what Browntree deduced about Abby being at the center of all of it was true, then maybe the Goners were like moths being drawn to a flame.

Abraham emerged a moment later. He shook his massive head. It rolled off his neck and slumped to one side. Ben saw that he had been hung—the noose was still around his neck, which was now barely attached to his head. Abraham flopped his head back into place.

"Where is she?" Alice asked.

"You tell me," Ben said.

Alice was on him faster than he could process it. She pushed him hard to the ground, although Ben couldn't be sure if she'd actually touched him.

"The Walker's daughter has something we need," Alice said. "And time has grown short. Wherever she is, we will find her."

"Then you don't need me, do you?" Ben asked. He wasn't sure where his brave words came from. Maybe it was because he was so scared that he'd come out the other side and simply couldn't be scared anymore. Or maybe it was because he'd seen so much and been through so many trials that he had no more fear in him. Whatever it was, he spoke with confidence and without flinching.

"Don't think for a moment I won't kill you," Alice said. "Or can't. There are other ways to lure her out of hiding."

Ben was about to reply when Leopold started saying something in German. Both Ben and Alice looked around. He held Abigail's note in one of his pale hands.

Alice bolted across the room and took the paper from Leopold's grip. She read it quickly and glanced up with much the same expression as Browntree.

"What's wrong?" Ben chided. "You look like you've seen a ghost."

"A most unpleasant thing this is," she said, ignoring Ben. "And most unexpected. She's gone to the Witch. She's giving herself up."

Leopold made a quizzical sound, while Baby Millie shrieked her displeasure.

"What does that mean?" Ben asked. "I mean, what does the Witch want with her? What do *you* want with her?"

"It's to be war, then?" Alice asked, brushing Ben's questions aside. "Well, war it shall be. Both the Walker and the daughter of the Walker will face their ends and *we* will deliver those ends. Half-breed or not, we will achieve our dominion without her."

Alice glanced at Ben, who had gotten up to his knees.

"There may be a use for you," she said. "And your companion, as well. I nearly had you last time, Walker's boy. This time, there is no fallen Goner to aid in your escape."

Ben stood up, angry and defiant.

"I'm not afraid anymore," he said. "I used to be, even last night. Now, well, what are you going to do to me? Kill me? I'm tired of all of this, anyway. I'd like to see my mother."

Alice laughed. It was a horrible sound, like razor blades down a chalkboard.

"If you want to see your mother, dying isn't the way you're going to do it," she said. "You think you have it all figured out, don't you? Alive and dead, either one or the other? You miss all the subtlety."

"What do you - -?" But before Ben could form the questions,

Abraham pulled him to his feet (and, yes, Ben certainly felt him), and pushed him out the door. Leopold took hold of Huck Browntree and they followed Ben and Abraham.

"Still think the Goners are a figment of my imagination?" Ben asked.

Browntree groaned. "I much preferred them in the abstract."

With the Goners hovering a few inches off the ground all around them, Ben and Huck headed into the woods to find Abby.

Chapter Nineteen

Sacrifice

Sunset Falls was a ghost town. In a sense, it had been since she and Ben had arrived. Now it truly lived up to that name. Abigail stood at the edge of the woods and surveyed the wreckage.

Whatever had been in the woods, whatever it was that Ben had heard, it had been real enough to lay waste to the town. The dozen buildings, the church, the general store, even "SPIRITS", were demolished. There was no evidence of natural phenomena—no fire, no wind, no earthquake. The forest not more than a half-dozen feet from the buildings, was as it had always been. What had been done to Sunset Falls had been done on purpose. The buildings were toppled. The church steeple lay sideways on the ground. Its bell was smashed in a jumble of sharp metal. A single large crack rose from the church basement to the top of its wall. The roof was gone. The general store, across the road, had crumbled. A strange smell hung in the air. It was like nothing Abby had ever smelled before. It was a combination of wood and decay—if she hadn't seen the town intact a few days earlier, she would have thought it had been this way for decades. The smell was like mustiness and age, but not quite. Something darker lived underneath. Abigail felt a wave of sadness wash over her. She was too late.

Abby walked past the church. The far wall had toppled. She could see the rows of pews inside.

"Hello?" she called. "Is anyone here?"

There was only silence. She kept walking. Her footsteps echoed through the empty town.

Then a sound, a scratching sound to her right. She looked over.

A storm cellar door opened. Abby fought the urge to run.

She recognized Reverend Martin from his tattered white priest's collar. He climbed out of the storm cellar and stood in front of the remains of his church.

"The prodigal returns," he said. He shook his head. His clothes were torn and a cut oozed on his exposed left knee. Abigail started to walk toward him, believing he might be the town's only survivor. She stopped when two more men emerged from the cellar. Her uncle Dutch glared at her.

"You coulda' stopped this," Dutch said. "'Cept you ran off to God knows where. Made it easy on yourself, but look at us. All the Witch wanted was you. Instead she took our town."

Abby stood silently and watched more people emerge from the cellar. Most she recognized, faces from the town. All the faces were angry, and directed their anger at her.

"You coulda done sometin'!" Dutch yelled.

"That's why I'm here now," Abby said.

Dutch looked at her with naked distrust. A crowd had gathered behind him now, a dozen strong and more emerging from underground. They murmured their surprise.

"What d'you mean t'do?" Dutch asked.

"Give myself up," Abigail said. An excited chatter went through the growing crowd.

"What does she mean?" Reverend Martin asked.

"I mean, I'm going to turn myself over to the Witch," Abby answered. "Sacrifice myself, I guess. Put an end to everything, once and for all."

"She's lying," a woman shouted from the crowd.

"It's a trick," a man added.

Reverend Martin held up his hand.

"Now, just a minute," he said. "We don't know the child's intentions. Perhaps she is tellin' the truth. You surely are, ain'tcha?"

"I said what I mean," Abby replied.

The reverend smiled. "Well, then, I'm mighty glad you've come to your senses."

Abigail narrowed her eyes. "It's not my senses I've come to, Reverend. I want my mother. Plain and simple. And I want whatever's poisoning this town to come to an end. Those two things are one in the same. Wherever my mother is, it's tied into the fate of Sunset Falls. And the fate of Sunset Falls is tied into my own. I didn't ask for this, any of it. But if I have some power to stop it, to bring my mother home or even just to let this awful little town not have to ring a bell at sunset, then I need to do it. I'm tired of running. And I'm tired of hiding. I'm not afraid anymore. I'm just tired."

Dutch shook his head and let out a soft chuckle.

"As noble as them words is, I think you're about a day late," he said. "Look at this town. Look at all'a'us. Shuttin' ourselves up unnergroun'. Livin' like we was bein' hunted."

"What choice do we have, Dutch?" Reverend Martin asked. "You're right, we ain't got much left of our town, but at least we're all still here. I ain't too certain that'll be the case after another night."

"It's too late, anyhow," Dutch said. "You heard what the Red Witch told us. There ain't no room left to negotiate."

"But that was before all of this," the reverend said. "And before the girl came to us. It changes everything. We take the girl to the Witch and then - -"

"No!" Dutch shouted. "Don't you unnerstan'? Whatever the Witch wanted from Abigail, she don't need it no more. Look at what happened to the town. Whatever it is she's got doin' her biddin' now, it sure looks a lot more powerful than some little girl who hears voices."

"She's all we got!" Reverend Martin argued.

"She ain't enough," Dutch said.

"This isn't up to you," Abby interjected. "I'm not even sure it's up to me anymore, either. Take me to the Red Witch. You know the way. Take me to the Witch and it's all over. Your town will be yours again, and no one'll need to be afraid. No matter what she wants from me, I'll make her leave. She'll go back to wherever she came from, and she'll let this town move on. Reverend, you know it's the only way."

Reverend Martin nodded.

"Tell me something," he asked. "Why do you care about the fate of our town? You and your brother can leave—an' you need never look back."

"My mother chose you," Abby replied. "That's as well as I can explain it. My mother chose you, and I choose you, too."

"It was different, when your mother was here," Reverend Martin said. "*We* were different, all of us. Happy. Alive. Not what you see today. Not this terrified group of victims. An' her bein' here made us even better. Even knowin' that she weren't one of us, weren't even really a human being, none of that mattered."

"She followed happiness," Abigail said. "And she found Sunset

Falls. Maybe you'll know what that's like again."

"We can only pray," Reverend Martin replied.

"Take me there," Abby said. "Please."

Reverend Martin put his hand on Abigail's shoulder as they walked through the woods. She shrugged it off. The feel of it made her sick. *He* made her sick, they all did. But she'd convinced them, and that was all that mattered. Dutch had nearly given her away, unwittingly, of course, but she'd had to think quickly. It wasn't for the sake of the town that she was going to the Witch. The town could rot and fall into the ground for all she cared. Her reason was more personal. Much more personal.

Things were following them. Shadows mostly, but lumbering ones. What Ben had seen, Abby mused. They had destroyed the town, the things from the woods. She wondered why they were letting them pass now. Perhaps it was the dappled sunlight—their strength came from fear, and fear was much more potent in the dark. But that wasn't the reason, and she knew it. It was her. Whatever power she had, it was keeping the fearsome things at bay. Barely.

Dutch was in the lead. He knew the path to the Witch's cabin well. Too well for Abigail's liking. There was more to Dutch than she knew. His deceit rolled off his body like fever. Try as she might, though, Abby couldn't figure it out. He was up to something, but what? And where was Aunt Penny? She should've been in the storm cellar with the others, but there had been no sign of her. And Dutch wasn't concerned. Either he knew where she was or he didn't care. Both of these options left Abby uneasy.

Leaves crunched under their feet. Autumn was coming. Already the shadows were lengthening. The days were getting shorter. The townspeople who followed behind them glanced nervously from side to side. There were too many shadows for their liking—too much like nighttime. And the rumblings from the forest were getting louder.

"How much farther?" Abby asked.

"Ain't far," Dutch replied. He didn't turn around, and instead continued marching with a purposeful stride.

"Were you in love with my mother, Dutch?" Abby asked. The idea struck her out of the blue, and the words were out of her mouth before she could consider them fully.

Dutch stopped. His shoulders stooped and he stood with his back to her for a long time.

"That's it, isn't it?" Abigail asked. "My God, that's really it. I can't believe you - -"

Dutch whirled around and grabbed her. He moved quicker than his age would have indicated, and he had both of her arms behind her back before she knew what had happened.

"This ends now," he hissed. "Not on your terms, on mine. Ain't no way I'm gonna' let her go for good. The Red Witch'll listen to me now. She's got to. I got what she wants."

Before Reverend Martin or anyone else could react, Dutch pulled Abigail deeper into the woods. The shadows around them pulsed with energy. Someone screamed, the same woman who'd called Abby a liar back in town. The forest erupted with silver light.

Abby recognized the Goners, the four of them who remained, but only by their clothes. They were something from nightmares now. They blew onto the path, Alice and Baby Millie, Abraham and Leopold. Instead of the floating silver bodies they once possessed, they were now made of a silver fire. Their faces, arms and legs, all of them but their clothes burned wildly. From the swirl of flames Abby glimpsed faces—not the faces of the Goners, but gruesome, terrifying faces, as if the flames of their bodies were actually windows into Hell itself. Angry, twisted forms writhed in the flames. Half-formed leathery skin, faces that melted and bubbled like lava, hands that were really claws, furious and tormented. Abigail screamed herself, and tried to break away from Dutch. His grip was iron and she couldn't get free.

"Give us the Walker's child!" Alice bellowed. It was her voice, Abby recognized it, but it was a hundred other voices, too. It was, in fact, as if all the voices Abby had been hearing suddenly spoke in unison.

Silver flame singed the trees. Smoke billowed from a fire started among the dead leaves. Abby choked and tried again to break away from Dutch. He held fast to her, desperate now.

"You cain't have her!" Dutch shrieked. His voice cracked like a teenage boy's. Abby smelled the sharp sting of urine as his bladder let go. She'd never seen someone so afraid, yet so determined not to be.

"Give us what is ours!" Alice boomed. The visions in the flames got worse, horrible things now, scenes of torture and murder and violent destruction. Abby saw a man's head ripped off, and a screaming baby gutted by a sword. A woman's hair was set on fire, and an old man was torn apart by dogs. She closed her eyes but it was inside her now, those awful visions. She couldn't escape them.

"Enough," a voice called. It was calm and not nearly as loud as the cacophony of the forest, yet it pierced the sound and instantly silenced it.

Abigail opened her eyes. The Goners had returned to normal (as normal as they'd ever been), and the flames and the visions in the flames were gone, too. In their place stood the Red Witch, small and round at the edge of the forest.

Abby almost laughed. The fury of the violent visions juxtaposed with the short, fat woman with the long black braid was nearly too much to bear. Yet her fear escalated. *This* was the real horror, not what the Goners had shown. This woman ran the show.

The small clearing was silent. The townspeople who had followed them cowered among the trees. Reverend Martin was on his knees. Dutch held tight to Abigail's arms, but a dark stain on his trousers indicated the state of things.

The Red Witch stepped forward. Her bare feet crinkled the leaves. There was no other sound. Even the Goners were silent.

"No one needs to be afraid of these amateur fear mongers," the Witch said. "These Goners are nothing but leftovers. Too stupid to die, too dead to live. All they have is fear."

"And what do you have?" Abigail asked. Terror clung to the roof of her mouth, but she swallowed it back.

"I have you," the Red Witch said. "And that's everything, isn't it?"

Dutch released his grip and pushed Abigail forward. She landed on her hands and knees between the Goners and the Witch.

"What am I, then?" Abby asked. "Come on, no more secrets. You won, right? At least let me know the truth."

"The truth?" the Witch asked. "The truth is a sliding scale. But I've already told you that."

"What's *your* truth, then?"

The Red Witch smiled. "My truth? *My* truth is that you are the mortal child of an immortal Walker. That makes you a conduit to all worlds. A tunnel, if you like. A doorway."

"Like those miners found at the end of the mine shaft?" Abigail asked.

"Only this doorway's not out of my reach," the Witch replied. "There are rules, you know."

"I've heard," Abby replied. "But why do you need a doorway? What's on the other side?"

The Red Witch looked at Abigail with an expression that bordered on sweetness.

"Freedom," she said.

"Freedom from what?"

"You wander the earth for a millennia, the scenery tends to look the same," the Witch said. "I want out. And you, my little Walker's child, are the key."

"There's where we end this," Alice said. For a moment, Abby had forgotten about the Goners. They hovered together now, more pale than silver.

"Your moment has passed," the Witch said. "Run along and stop scaring people."

Alice seethed. Beneath her silver clothing, her pale body trembled. Then, like a balloon being inflated, her torso expanded. A burst of concussive energy surged from her body. The Red Witch tumbled to the ground. A cyclone of dead leaves followed in her wake.

"The Walker's child is mine!" Alice roared. The other Goners rallied around her. Baby Millie shrieked.

The Red Witch leaped to her feet. Abby didn't believe it at first, that a creature so round and awkward could be so agile. The Witch was on her feet in a heartbeat, and released a burst of energy that made Alice ripple. The Goner went limp.

Baby Millie shrieked again, a death howl, and set a shock wave of her own toward the Red Witch. The Witch buckled but didn't topple, and threw a burst of her own at Baby Millie. The Goner split in half, rippled, and then came back together.

Abigail felt a hand on her shoulder. She turned to knock Reverend Martin away and was face-to-face with Benjamin.

"Time to go," he said.

"No!" Abby yelped.

"What do you mean, no?"

"You won't understand."

"Try me."

Abby groaned. "Mom's alive, Ben. I feel it. And the Red Witch is the only way to get to her."

"Then we'll find her together," Ben said. "Without the Witch. Look, if what they say about you is true, then you don't need them. *They* need *you*."

"Ben, Mom's so close I can smell her," Abby said. "She's here. I've got to find her."

"That's why you left me?" Ben asked. "C'mon, Abby, you can't keep this stuff from me. Let me help you. Let *us* help you, me and Huck."

"He's here, too?"

"He's on his way back to his cabin," Ben said. "Where we're going."

All around them, the Goners were locked in combat with the Red Witch. Abraham dealt her a powerful blow, but she recovered almost instantly, and sent the noose-necked Goner reeling. Alice was back, too, although not to her full cocky demeanor. She had enough strength, though, to send out a radiating blast of energy that knocked down everyone in the clearing, Red Witch and townspeople alike. Ben took his opportunity and pulled Abby into the woods.

Chapter Twenty

Dutch Comes Clean

Huck was in his cabin, salvaging what he could. Most of the instruments were smashed, but he managed to find some undamaged components. He was so engrossed in what he was doing that he didn't even flinch when Ben and Abby burst through the door.

"What happened in here?" Abby asked.

"The Goners," Huck said. "This is what they were doing while we were busy running away."

"I'm sorry, Huck," Abby said.

Huck glanced up and shook his bushy head. He brushed away his emotions.

"No matter," he said. "It's past. What is of paramount importance now is figuring out what all this is about."

"And how to stop it," Ben added.

"Of course, yes," Huck said.

"Abby, tell him about Mom," Ben insisted.

"Come on, Ben, let's not - -" Abby began, but Huck cut her off.

"Your mother, eh?" he asked. "She is at the center of the whole thing, isn't she? And you as well."

"Tell him why you ran away this morning."

"Ben, knock it - -"

"Yes, running off was a foolish thing to do," Browntree replied. "If not for your brother here, who knows what fate would have befallen you."

"It's nice to see you're back to normal," Abby quipped.

"What is that supposed to mean?" Huck asked.

"It means coming back to your lab seems to have made you a pompous ass again."

"And you're still behaving like a petulant child," he shot back. "But none of this is getting us any closer to solving the problem."

Abby threw up her hands. "Why do you think that this "problem", as you call it, *can* be solved? It's not some experiment run wild, you know. There's a very real force out there, manifesting itself into some very real things. The town is in ruins. Did you know that? Fear doesn't topple buildings. Fear doesn't destroy things. Fear is an emotion, it's a *reaction* to those things."

"But don't you see?" Huck argued. "Fear *is* the reason for all of this. That's becoming clearer every day."

"Not to me!"

"Then you're not opening your eyes!" Huck flashed. He took a breath, and softened.

"We *perceive* our reality, Abigail," he said. "Not experience it. We interpret what we're seeing and smelling and tasting and touching and then pour it through the filter of our minds. Something that is completely normal to me can send you into fits because of your perception of it. We each color our own experiences with the shades of our own prejudices."

"I understand that, but what's happening isn't perception," Abby replied. "It's fear, all right, but it's *real* fear. There's really something out there to be afraid of."

"But what if there isn't?" Huck asked. "What if all that's happening is simply happening because this town if terrified? Plain and simple, out-and-out terrified?"

"How come Ben and I are seeing it, then?" Abby asked. "And you, for that matter?"

"It's the accepted reality," Huck replied. "On some level, simply by being here, simply by living among the prevailing energy, we have become part of it, begun to accept it as our own reality."

"You're saying, then, that the Red Witch isn't real?"

"No, I'm sure she's entirely real," Huck said. "And I will even assume that what she's told you is true. Perhaps there are Walkers, creatures that need human emotion to survive and who wander from place to place in search of it. As ridiculous as I would have thought that even a few days ago, it doesn't seem so far-fetched now."

"Why not?"

"Because of you," he said. "Because of the readings I've taken of you."

"Sorry?"

"Your electromagnetic energy is simply off the chart, Abigail, even when you're sleeping. It's impossible for a human being to carry that kind of energy and be alive. Sure, if Ben or I touch a doorknob, we'll discharge some energy in the form of static. But you, you're a swirling *ball* of energy. It's impossible. And that's how I know there's something to this."

Abby furrowed her brow. "You're studying me, then?"

Huck rolled his eyes. "I'm not dissecting you or anything like that. They're just tests. You weren't even aware I was performing them. Mostly when you were asleep in the mine tunnel."

"Asleep?"

"The point is, this is real. That part of it, anyway. It's provable."

"Tell him about Mom," Ben said.

"Ben, please."

"What about your mother?" Huck asked.

"She's alive," Ben said.

"Ben!" Abby flashed. On a far table, a glass beaker shattered. All three of them looked at it, dumbfounded.

"It's starting, then," Huck said.

"What's starting?" Abby asked.

Huck ran a hand through his hair. "It's just theory, mind you, conjecture, really, but I have a supposition that we're nearing a flashpoint."

"What kind of flashpoint?" Abby asked.

"A big one," Huck said. "A boiling over, as it were. There is so much fear energy, and who knows what other kind of energy, building and building over this town that something simply must give. Last night, what happened to the town, the destruction you mentioned, I believe that was the beginning. But something is continuing to build. Even my most rudimentary electronybmic sensing devices, the ones not in a hundred pieces, anyway, are sensing this spike in energy. I can even imagine those voices you hear are getting stronger, too."

Abby lowered her eyes. "One is."

"Tell us," Huck said.

"The voices have gotten louder, you're right," Abby began. "And I've largely been able to ignore them. But last night, in the middle of the night, I heard one voice so clearly it startled me awake."

"Your mother," Huck said.

"Yes," Abby replied. "It was as clear as if she was standing over my bed like she used to do when I was a little kid, back in my own bed. I could *smell* her, it was that real. She told me it was true, that she was a Walker, and that she was still alive. Trapped, though. Captive, she called it."

"Captive? Held by whom?" Huck asked.

"She didn't tell me," Abby replied. "And I didn't ask. I was too much in shock. She told me to help her, that only I could do it."

"And that's why you left," Huck said.

"Yes. I'm sorry."

"Apologize to your brother, not to me," Huck replied. "He's the only one who put himself at risk."

Abigail glanced over at Ben. He looked bigger than before, taller, stouter. A man instead of a boy. She wanted to tell him that, but the look in his eye scared her off. She'd hurt him again, and badly this time. He'd come to find her but he'd changed in the process. His heart was closing itself off. Scarring over, perhaps, from too many of her wounds. Too many times of her running off and leaving him alone. She wanted to apologize, but where could she begin? Some apologies were just too big to make.

"She's alive out there," Abby said. "Or somewhere. And the Witch is the only way we can find her."

"If my theory of a coming flashpoint is true, then being near the Red Witch when it happens is probably a bad idea," Huck said. "Ben did the right thing by collecting you and bringing you here. With the Goners otherwise occupied, we're able to regroup without fear of being - -"

As he said it, though, the front door of his cabin burst open. Dutch flew threw the door, yelling incoherently. He grabbed Abigail and pulled her toward the door.

"Let me go!" Abby shrieked.

"I want her back!" Dutch cried. "You're gonna' get her back for me!"

Huck moved to block their way out, but Dutch brushed him aside with one powerful hand. Abigail fought like a cat but Dutch was stronger than all of them. All around the cabin, glass was breaking. Windows and beakers alike shattered.

"You're the devil," Dutch said. "You're your Mama's shadow, you is."

"Get your hands off me!" Abby hollered, and then as if he'd suddenly come to his senses, Dutch released her. For a moment he grinned an idiot grin. Then he crumpled to the floor, unconscious. Abby looked at the place where he'd stood. Ben was there now, holding a large black frying pan and looking down at Uncle Dutch at his feet.

It took a long time for Dutch to come around. In the end, it was the smelling salts Huck kept in his cupboard that did the trick. Dutch coughed and sputtered like he'd been underwater. He slowly focused on the trio around him.

They'd tied him to a chair. Perhaps it was overkill, the copious amounts of rope they'd used, but Huck supposed they couldn't be too careful.

"Who hit me?" Dutch asked.

"I did," Ben replied.

Dutch squinched his face into a painful grin.

"Good arm," he said.

"Thanks, I guess."

"It's time to talk, Dutch," Abby said. "You've told me a bit, now tell us the rest. The whole story this time, not just what's convenient to you."

Abigail pulled one of the ropes tighter and Dutch howled in pain.

"Aw'right, yes, I loved your Ma," he said. "She weren't like nothin' we'd ever seen here before. Nothin' *I'd* ever seen before. 'Cause it was personal by then. I din't care 'bout how the rest of the town felt about her. I only knew I loved her an' I had to make her love me, too.

"We knew what she was. She din't make no secret about it. Said she trusted us, knew she could trust mountain folk. We was good-hearted, she said. That's why she'd come in the first place, she said. 'Cept I don't think that was the whole reason. She came here like she had a reason t'do it, y'know? Some people you see 'em an' they just mosey along, ain't got no destination an ain't in no hurry t'get there. Your Mama weren't like that. She had a sparkle in her eye like she knew herself a good ol' juicy secret, one she was just bustin' t'tell.

"She found Galen near as soon as she got here. He was a handsome man, my brother was, fierce handsome, but that weren't why she seeked him out. It was his kindness, and his love. His *ability* t'love, more'n that. Galen was quiet an' straightforward an' as true as the settin' sun. Your Mama fell in love with him, if love is even possible with her kind."

"Her kind?" Abby asked.

Dutch nodded. "Them Walkers ain't like normal folks. Your Mama put on a good show for you kids, I'm sure she did, but feelin's wasn't really their thing. Walkers, they're like chameleon lizards almost, the kind that changes colors dependin' on what they're sittin' on? Anyways, Molly took her feelin's from what was around her. If we was happy, she was real happy. If we was a little down, you could see her change, like it was physically affectin' her. Good thing for her there was lots t'be happy about in them days. We was a minin' town then, an' we was thrivin'. Not too many people comin' in t'disturb us, so we could live our lives the way we wanted. Lots of money, too, though ain't nobody had much use for it then. Everything we wanted was here in our valley. Your Mama just made everything better."

"Did you tell my mother how you felt about her?" Abigail asked.

Dutch shook his head. "She knew, though. Same way she knew 'bout most everything. Had a knack of askin' the right question, like you did when you asked if I loved her."

"What did she say to you?"

"Oh, she let me down easy, said it was a natural thing, that it happened to her all the time 'cause of what she was, but that it just wouldn't work out. That's 'fore I knew 'bout her an' Galen. 'Fore the mine, too."

"The mine?"

"The door at the end of the mine shaft," Dutch said. "It changed everything. *That's* what started it all, not your Mama. She was long gone by then, anyways. Married your Pa and left us far behind. It was them damn fools that opened that door. I knew 'em all, too. Ralph Williams, Doc McCutcheon, we called him 'Doc' 'cause he could fix damn near everything. Jimmy Burroughs, Conrad Bates. It's a tiny little town an' everybody knows everybody's business. I knew them boys like I knew my own kin. They was always damn fools, the lot of 'em. Reckless, too. Had to be to go into them mines every day. Wouldn't'a thought twice about openin' the door. I'm sure they musta' had a bad feelin' about it. Billy Corrigan, the one who got out, he even said so 'fore he died. But they opened it anyway. An' that's when it all started."

"What started?" Ben asked.

"All'a this," Dutch replied, and shook his head. "The dark days. Look, I know you cain't imagine this place no different than it is now. Or *me* any different than I am now. But it changed. *I* changed. What came outta' that mine did it, not your Mama."

"What was it?" Abby asked. "How did it start?"

"Nothin' happened at first," Dutch said. "Nothin' we could see, at least. When Billy Corrigan stumbled out of the mine, we was all at Lily Cartwright's weddin'. Most of us, anyways. It was a good weddin'. Lily an' her man, Daniel McCormick, they was both young an' in love. They was gonna' start farmin' some land other side of the valley. Danny'd worked for me a spell an' learned how t'do it. He was good, too, near good as me. Folks said if anyone could make things grow outta' this earth, they had t'be good. Danny coulda' done it, too. They had themselves a good life stretchin' out in front of 'em. An' we all… we was all proud. Then Billy Corrigan opened up that chapel door an' everything changed."

"What happened?"

"He was bloodied up an' tore up, too, real bad. Ain't even sure how he had the strength t'make it back t'town. He fell into your Aunt Penny's arms, she was the first one t'stand up an' she caught him, kept him from fallin'. The boy started babblin' about everybody dyin' an' something awful killin' 'em faster'n they could run. He weren't clear about that, but he was clear about one thing."

"What was that?" Abby asked.

"They'd found a door at the end of the tunnel, a tunnel they'd just fresh dug out. Said it weren't possible but they'd found it, anyhow. A big metal door, with all manner of designs on it. Penny told Corrigan t'draw out what he'd seen, an' he did it on the floor of the church, usin' his own blood for ink. I never seen nothin' so sad as that. Desperate, too. That boy knew he din't have much time. Whatever'd happened to him was gettin' worse. His hair turned white right there in front of us all. None of us could believe it, but we all seen it. So Corrigan drew out a couple of the shapes he'd seen right there on the floor. Then Billy Corrigan looked up at Penny with them big wide brown eyes of his an' smiled this godawful bloody smile an' said, 'we let 'em loose, Penny. God help us, we did.' Then he died with that bloody smile still on his face."

"What happened after that?" Ben asked.

"Oh, it was all over," Dutch said. "Your Mama an' Paw, they was already gone. Left in the night, didn't tell no one. I knew by then that she'd lied to me 'bout how lovin' me just wouldn't work out, it weren't done with her kind. I assumed it was any mortal man she couldn't love. I thought maybe it was 'cause of Penny. Turns out she di'n't love me. They left 'fore they had you. Not long, though. Galen wrote us some. Sent along photographs, like everything was all still all right between us. Even brought you t'see us one time, you might even remember that.

"Weren't too long after Molly left that the good days left, too. Whatever came outta' that mine tunnel, she knew it was comin'. It hit her hard. An' her goin' left us all wide open for the darkness to fall."

"You mean fear?" Huck asked. Dutch glared at him, perhaps having forgotten he was there. Dutch nodded.

"Fear was the big one," Dutch said. "Terror, more'n that, even. The woods around us came t'life. Places we'd seen all our lives, places we'd played in as kids, for God's sake, it all changed. It was like a shadow fell over us, 'cept this shadow came from down below."

"The Red Witch," Abby said.

"She came after your Mama left, maybe a three years, maybe four," Dutch replied. "Not out of the mines, though. She just wandered into town like she owned it. She was a Walker, too, we knew that the moment we saw her. An' maybe we hoped she'd bring back some of what your Mama took with her. Di'n't take long t'realize the Red Witch was a whole different breed."

Abby lowered her eyes and ran a hand through her red hair.

"There's one more thing," Dutch said, "long as I'm bein' honest."

Abby looked up. "What is it?" she asked.

"After things had been goin' bad such a long time, me an' some of the others from town, Reverend Martin, Dick Maloney, Dalton Freewald, we decided t'try t'make us a deal with the Witch. Figure out some way t'pull our town back from the brink of what was gonna' happen to it. All four of us went, but it was only me who went inside. Maybe if it'd been one of the others, who knows…"

"What did you do?"

"The Red Witch has a knack for knowin' what we're thinkin'," Dutch continued. "Even if we ain't even fully aware of it ourselves. She knew I loved your Ma, an' I think that's why she brought me in alone. I know it is, 'cause no one else had the same kinda' connection. I never stopped lovin' your Ma. The Red Witch used that connection to take your Ma away."

"No!" Abigail shouted.

"The Witch sent out some kind of voodoo to your Mama, suckin' the good right outta' her an' leavin' her t'die. 'Cept them Walkers cain't die, not like normal folks. Their bodies might blow away, but you're right t'believe you're Mama's alive, little girl. Ain't possible for her t'be any other way. At least not 'lest she chooses to."

"Chooses?" Abby asked. "What do you - -?"

"The Witch di'n't want your Mama, she wanted you," Dutch said. "You're the doorway to her next world. She told you that herself. She's ready t'move on. She cain't go through the door in the mine tunnel, hell if I know why, but she can go through you. Them voices you hear, the ones gettin' louder? Those are voices from the other side. Might even be voices from a *lot* of other sides. You're a special sort of creature, Abigail. The perfect mix of human bein' an' Walker. A once in a lifetime sorta' thing. That's why they're all drawn t'you like moths. The Witch, the Goners, even them things what live in the tunnels. They want to use you t'move between the worlds. They cain't do it themselves, no matter how powerful they are in this world. An' they hate you for that. They'll use whatever they can to get control of your abilities. Me. Your brother. Even your Ma. But your Daddy, he knew what he was doin', sendin' you here."

"Dad knew about all of this?" Abby asked.

"'Course he did,' Dutch said. "He'd'a been a fool had he not, an' your daddy weren't no fool. He knew what'd happened to your Ma, an' he knew you was the only one who could find her."

"But where is he?" she asked. "If he knows, why isn't he here?"

"He's searchin', same as you," Dutch replied. "Followin' your Mama's trail, seekin' out the other Walkers an' tryin' to find another way in."

"In?"

"To where your Mama is."

"Then I've gotta' find her," Abby said. She looked first at Huck, then at Ben. "*We've* got to find her."

Ben smiled sadly, and nodded his head.

"I think I know who can help us," he said.

Chapter Twenty-One

The Truth, Plain & Ugly

It was completely dark by the time they reached the Falls. Ben was in the lead. Huck and Abby followed close behind. They'd left Dutch in the cabin, bound and gagged. It seemed cruel, but both Abby and Ben felt safer with their uncle out of the way.

The sun had set and the moon had not yet risen. The only light came from the stars, and from a faint silver-blue glow on the riverbank.

"I hoped you'd come," Augustus Dolarhyde said.

"We hoped you'd be here," Ben replied. He tried not to look shocked, but Gus was in bad shape. He was only silver in the broadest sense. His glow had faded to a burnished blue, and he was almost completely transparent. He had wounds all over his body, deep cuts that would have killed a living person, but on Gus' disembodied body, they appeared only as dark holes.

"I know how I look," Gus said. He managed a wan smile.

"Who did this to you?" Abigail asked.

"The Goners," he said. "It's always the Goners, isn't it? The worst thing is, I had a choice. After my accident on the farm back home, I wandered for a long time. I ended up on a road, and at a fork in the road I found them. Or rather, they found me, because I think they were waiting. They told me I could go back to the world that I knew. I remember standing at that crossroads looking at them, at Alice, and then looking the other way. There was no one there to meet me. I thought there would be. Isn't that what they say about dying, that you'll be greeted by your loved ones? No one was there, only the Goners. I didn't think death would be so lonely. That's why I followed them."

Ben knelt down beside him. Gus sat cross-legged, but floated a few inches off the ground.

"What'll happen to you now?" Ben asked.

"There's not much left of me," Gus replied. "I'm fading all the time. It's been hard to stay here this long. I'll disappear, I suppose. Just wink out like I wasn't even here."

"Gus, come on, there's got to be something we can - -" Ben began, but Gus cut him off.

"There's nothing to be done, and time is short," he said. "You need to know about your mother. The truth about her, because, contrary to what Professor Browntree believes, there *is* empirical truth."

Abby sat down beside her brother.

"Tell us," she said.

"Your mother, a Walker, came to the town of Sunset Falls, attracted by its positive energy. It called to her, as it were. But she also came with a purpose of her own. An agenda, I guess you'd call it."

"What did she want?" Abby asked.

Gus looked at her sharply. Even though he was barely there, barely even visible to her, his eyes still held some real power.

"When we discover the truth about those we love, we also shatter our myths about them," he said. "But if you remember that your mother is only what she is, and that everyone, human beings, Walkers, everyone is doing the best they know how to do, you can begin to accept her decisions as her own."

"What is that supposed to - -?"

"Your mother wanted to cross over," Gus said. "As much if not more than the Red Witch. She was tired of wandering, like I was when I found the Goners. Your mother had Walked for a long time, and it was long past her time to fade away. But that isn't something a Walker can do. They're cursed, in a way, because they can't stop Walking. Your mother saw a way out and she decided to take it."

"Me," Abby said.

"Exactly," Gus replied. "You were born to be destroyed, so that she could move on to another realm. You have reached your sixteenth year, the age at which you were to be… harvested, I suppose, is the best way to describe it. That's why the Red Witch took your mother when she did. She wanted you. And that's why your father sent you here. He wants your mother back."

"And the Goners?" Abigail asked.

"They just want to move on."

Abby stood up. "Why did you tell me this? I don't want to know it!"

"I didn't recognize my choice when I was faced with it," Gus replied. "I'm giving you yours. Walk away now, you and your brother, and never come back. Don't search for your mother, don't search for your father, and live your lives in obscurity."

"That's not much of a choice," Abby said. "What's my alternative?"

"Go find your mother."

"But I don't know where she is."

Gus smiled wryly. "Of course you do."

Abby realized then that she *did* know, she'd known all along.

"The door," she said. "In the mine tunnel. That's the way in, isn't it?"

Gus nodded. "But going in doesn't mean you're coming out. Your mother means to cross over. So does the Red Witch. So do the Goners, and everything else that was released through that door and then trapped on this side. Search your own heart and find out what you want from your mother. Can she give it to you? Everything you knew was a myth, Abigail. Think about why you want to find her. Is it for you to move on into the future, or to hold onto the past?"

Abby lowered her eyes.

"All I've wanted since she died was another day," she said. "A perfect kind of day, running in the park and the sound of her laughing… and the smell of her hair. I miss her so terribly."

"And now?" Gus asked.

"Now I just don't know."

"Loving someone is a hard thing," Gus said. "And missing someone is harder still."

"Knowing the truth is harder than it all," Abby said, and sighed. "What do I do?"

Gus shook his head. "That's your decision. Even if I wanted to, I couldn't make it for you. Neither can your brother. All anyone can do is help you follow through with it."

Abigail wiped tears from her eyes. She hadn't cried for a long time, and didn't want to start now.

"My time is over now," Gus said. Even as he spoke he faded further, becoming barely perceptible against the gloom.

"Listen to your soul, Abigail," he said. "That's the one thing that can't be fooled."

And then he was gone, and Ben and Abby and Huck were alone at the waterfall. They were quiet for a time, listening to the water roiling past.

"What do we do now?" Ben asked.

Abby shook her head. "We make a decision," she said, and snorted. "Or, according to the ghost, *I* make a decision."

Abigail whirled on Huck. "You're being uncharacteristically quiet. What's your take? I mean, as our resident electromagnetologist or whatever you are. Things still pretty clear-cut for you?"

"Get angry with me if you wish, but it won't make your decision any easier," Huck replied.

"I didn't ask for this!" Abby yelled. "Do you hear me? I didn't ask for it, and I don't want it!"

Ben stood up beside her and put his hand on her shoulder.

"I'll do whatever you say," he said. "If you want to leave, I'll leave with you. If you want to stay and see what's behind that door, I'll do that, too."

Abby's fury ebbed. She looked down at her brother with affection.

"You've been beside me the whole way, Benji," she said. "Finding me when I ran away, calling me back when I've gone too far. And all I do is rain all over you. Why do you keep coming back? Even though I keep pushing you away, somehow you always find me again."

Ben smiled as if the question itself was ridiculous.

"You're my family," he said. "And no matter what you do, no matter where you go, you'll always be a part of me. You can keep pushing me away but I won't stay far. You don't have to be nice to me, because that's not what it's about. *I* love *you*. It doesn't matter if you love me. It'd be nice if you said it once in a while, but I'll live. 'Cause it doesn't matter what I get in return. I can't help the fact that I love you. We've got a history together. And no matter what you do, you'll always be my sister."

"And she'll always be our Mom," Abby said, and hugged her brother tight. "Thanks for that, Ben."

"As warm and fuzzy as this all leaves me," Huck said, "we have a very real problem in getting to the end of the tunnel."

"How so?" Ben asked.

"The miners, remember?" Huck said. "How do we know that what happened to them won't happen to us?"

"We don't," Abby replied.

"So we're going back into those tunnels, all the way to the end, knowing that it is not only potentially but also quite likely lethal?" he asked.

Abby smiled and shook her head.

"You worry too much," she said. Ben laughed. It was a good sound this time, and they both felt a little of the weight lift.

"In or out, Browntree?" Abby asked.

"Well, in, of course," Huck was flustered. "Just wanted to get all the facts before I did something reckless, that's all. You'd be well advised to do the same now and then."

"We need lamps and probably ropes, too," Abby said.

"What about shovels?" Ben asked.

"Yeah, good idea."

Huck sighed, resigned. "We lost most of that in the tunnels last time, but I've got a few extras in my cabin."

They followed Huck through the woods as the bright crescent moon rose over the hills.

Chapter Twenty-Two
The Miners Have Their Say

They stood at the mouth of the Archer mine. It was a different entrance than either Ben or Abby and Huck had used. At one time, there had been an attempt to seal this entrance off. Splintered wooden boards littered the gravel path in front of the tunnel. Whatever had been sealed in had gotten loose—but they knew that already. The evidence of it was all around them.

"Are you ready?" Ben asked.

"No," Abby replied, and grinned.

"What's funny?"

"Absolutely nothing," she said. "Isn't that a hoot?"

"Not really."

"I don't think so, either."

"Now or never, kids," Browntree said. Abigail looked at him questioningly. She'd forgotten how much older he was. From the moment she'd stepped into his cabin, they'd been peers. Now, with his awkward attempt at authority, she saw the streaks of gray in his hair, and the deep lines around his eyes and mouth. He was their father's age, maybe even older. That realization made her wonder about his history, and the events that had brought him to Sunset Falls. Did he have a family? Kids? If he did, where were they? And if he didn't, did he want them?

"What's wrong?" he asked. Abby shook her head and looked away. Her questions would be out of place—they were a distraction and now was definitely not the time to be distracted. She sighed and steeled herself.

"Let's go," she said. Abby didn't wait for the others to follow. Ben and Huck were close behind. They stepped carefully over the broken boards.

It was cool inside the tunnel. The temperature dropped steeply as soon as they stepped in.

"Strange," Huck said.

"What?" Abigail asked.

"The drop in temperature," he replied. "Uncharacteristic. Anything underground, cave or mine, has a constant temperature. It's stable. *Measurable*. This, well, it almost feels like a breeze, except I can't feel any air moving."

"Maybe there's a vent down the tunnel, like we got out through before?" Ben suggested.

Abby shook her head. "Come on, Ben, we all know what it is."

Ben exhaled heavily. Steam puffed out in front of him.

"It's getting colder in here," Huck said.

"It knows we're in here," Abby asserted.

"What knows we're in here?" Ben asked.

"Whatever's been waiting for me all this time," Abby replied. She turned to face her companions.

"Look, maybe it's better if only I go on ahead," she said. "This whole damn thing seems to be centered around me, doesn't it? And you've both already put yourselves into enough peril already. Maybe it'd just be better if - -"

"Shut up, Abigail," Ben said. Abby lowered her eyes and smiled a little to herself. She didn't want to go through this alone, no matter how noble it sounded. She took her brother's small, grubby hand and held it tightly in her own.

"I know I haven't said it enough, Benny, but I - -"

"Don't," he replied. "It's okay. You don't need to. I'd be following you even if you punched me in the nose and left me in the corner."

"I don't think it'll come to that," she said. "Huck?"

"If I left now, I'd never know, would I?" he replied. "Lead the way."

Abby did just that, the heavy flashlight casting the mine tunnel into stark and shadowy relief. Their shadows danced across the wooden support beams. Somewhere, water dripped. The sound added to the loneliness of the place. Abigail wanted to go home. And not just to Dutch and Penny's minimum security prison, but home home, back to the city, to the apartment on Bleeker Street where Mom had taught her how to sew a button on a shirt and Dad had come home tired and happy and they'd sung strange Appalachian songs and little Benji had thumped his feet on the floor to the beat. Things had been right then, good, when Mom was only the sweet-smelling woman who made cookies and kissed whatever hurt and made it stop hurting. Mom was someone else now, a monster who had cursed this town and even her own daughter, a monster herself born simply to be destroyed. What kind of monster was her mother? A cold one, Abby knew. Nearly as cold as the tunnel had become.

No, she was doing it again. She had to stop. Twisting her mind with worry only distracted her from what was happening now. And besides, what could she do about any of it? Her mother was what she was, and those days of singing and happiness, they were gone. All of it was over, and nothing would be the same. Abby knew she'd have to accept that. Her survival now demanded it. Knowing it, though, didn't make it any easier. Nothing made it easier.

"What's that?" Ben shone his light ahead of hers, and higher. Abby and Huck followed his gaze.

"It's a cave-in," Abby said.

"No, it's not," Huck countered.

"Well, it sure *looks* like a cave-in," Abby argued.

"It's a wall," Ben said, "Isn't it?"

Huck nodded. "It's too symmetrical to be a cave-in. Look, the stones are placed just so. And it's relatively flat, too, straight up and down. If it was a cave-in, there would be more debris at the bottom and less at the top."

"Yeah, I see now," Abby said. "But what do you suppose it's doing here?"

"Maybe the townspeople put it up," Huck suggested. ""They sure barricaded the entrance pretty well."

Ben shook his head. "Something slammed through that one," he said. "But this wall's still in one piece."

"What if it was the miners?" Abby asked.

"This barricade is still intact, like Ben said," Huck replied. "If, in fact, we assume this to be a barricade."

"What else could it be?" Ben asked.

"So why isn't this one smashed, too?" Huck asked, ignoring Ben's question. "If the wood that had been nailed over the entrance back there had been broken, and from the inside, and if the miners who discovered the door built this, then why is this wall still intact?"

"Because whatever it was that broke through the wooden barricade outside was already in this part of the tunnel when the miners built their wall," Abby said.

"So what's on the other side?" Ben asked.

"That's the million-dollar question, isn't it?" Huck replied.

"There's only one way to find out," Abby said.

Huck raised an eyebrow. "Go through it?"

"I don't see any other options," Abby said. "Besides, there might be something on the other side of this wall that lets us know what happened."

"Maybe there's a good reason this wall is here," Ben said.

Abby flashed. "And maybe there's a good reason we've got to break it down."

"I just meant - -"

"Are you in or out, Benji?" she asked. "'Cause I have a feeling that whatever's on the other side of this, we're gonna' need to be committed to get through."

"I said I'm in," Ben muttered.

"Huck?"

"Right behind you, just being the voice of reason," he said.

"I think I've heard all the reason I can handle," Abby replied. "Come on, let's pull this thing down."

They did it with their bare hands, starting at the top. Huck suggested doing it that way, to avoid having it collapse into an impassable rubble pile. The stones were stacked tightly together, but without mortar between them. Once they worked the first stone out, the three of them made short work of the rest of the wall. In under a half hour, they'd cleared an opening they could squeeze through.

"It smells," Ben said. Huck sniffed the air.

"Sulphur," he observed. "And something rotten."

Abby picked up her flashlight and stepped through the hole. She shone her light around the tunnel.

"Nothing in here but—oh, God!" she screamed. Huck and Ben both tried to push their way through the opening together. Ben won out and was at his sister's side in a moment.

"What is it?" he asked. Abby shone her dimming flashlight to the left.

Three bodies lay against the tunnel wall. They were all badly decomposed, mostly skeletal but still clinging to some of their flesh. The smell of rot was stronger on this side of the rock wall. Ben gagged for a moment, then composed himself.

"I kinda' wish they'd just been skeletons," Abby said.

"Not warm enough in here," Huck replied. "Not moist enough, either. Their decomposition is taking its sweet time."

"They're the miners, aren't they?" Ben asked.

"I think so," Abby said. "Some of them, anyway."

"Where are the rest?" Ben asked.

"Probably didn't make it this far," Huck replied. "I think we're beginning to get a clearer picture, though."

"What do you mean?" Abby asked.

"They built this wall," Huck said. "To seal off the tunnel. Why they sealed themselves in, too, I don't know. But it was effective. The wall held."

"What about the broken boards at the entrance?"

"Something had gotten ahead of them," Huck surmised. "Maybe it was trapped in here, too. Not able to leave the mine tunnel until just recently. Or maybe it was one of the Goners. Who knows? The point is, the people from town boarded up the mine. These miners wanted a more permanent barricade."

"For what reason?" Abby asked. "What were they trying to keep in here?"

"Look, one of them has something in his hand," Ben said.

Abby stepped over to the dead miners. Up close, the smell was even worse. It stung her nose and made her eyes water. She bent down. The miners' faces looked like blackened cottage cheese. The one she was closest to, the one in the middle who held a small book, had two crushed holes where his eyes had been. Abby tried not to look at them, but it was hard to avoid them. The empty sockets had a grotesque allure. She reached down and put her hand around the book.

It grabbed her hand. The thing's fingers were bony but strong. She tried to pull away but it held her tight. Then it opened its mouth.

"Your Mama's with us, Abigail," it said. Its voice was like gritty razor blades.

"Let go of me!" she yelled.

"You're gonna' die down here, too," the dead miner said.

Abigail pulled hard on the small book. The dead man's hand tightened around her own. Then with a snap she broke its fingers off. Momentum sent her flying across the tunnel. She hit her head on the rock, and was momentarily stunned.

The dead miner started to get up. His body made a gelatinous fart as its liquefied insides shifted.

Ben ran forward, pulling a shovel from Huck's backpack. He stabbed the shovel's blade into the dead miner's neck, and its rotten head rolled across the mineshaft. The miner stopped moving and crumpled to its dead knees.

Abby pried the miner's hand off her wrist. The decomposed stump had no strength anymore. She tossed it aside. Abby looked down at the palm-sized leather book she held in her hand. It was tied together with a frayed string.

"Is everyone okay?" Huck asked. He shone his light over their pale faces. Abigail nodded but Ben didn't acknowledge him.

"Benji?" Abigail called. "You all right?"

"It was dead," he muttered. "It was dead and then it *grabbed* you, and I had to chop its head off."

"I know, Ben," Abby said. "I think we're gonna' see a lot of impossible things before this is all over. Pull it together, okay?"

Ben glanced up. "Yeah, yeah, sure. I'm okay."

Abby nodded and held up the book.

"Anyone for some light reading?" she asked.

Huck pulled their packs across the tunnel, away from the remaining dead miners. He kept his light trained on them, sensitive to any movements they might make. Ben crawled over to Abby and huddled close. She untied the string that bound the leather book and let it fall to the floor. She turned the first page.

"It's a diary," she said. "It's just everyday stuff, though, nothing about what happened in - -" She flipped through the pages. "Oh, wait, here, yeah. It starts here."

"Read it," Huck ordered.

"It starts off, 'May 10. I don't know what we've found. Dug out a door, a heavy metal door, looks like it should be in a castle. Deke wanted to open it. The rest of us wasn't sure. We all had real bad feelings about it. Most of us wanted to turn and run. Deke wouldn't move, said we had to open it. Jimmy Duncan argued with him, and Deke raised up a pry bar like he was gonna' strike him. We was all afraid. I had a hard time keepin' my bladder from letting go. The door was stuck but the lot of us finally got it to open. When we did, Deke stepped inside. We couldn't stop him. It was dark. Then something flashed, two big red eyes. Deke screamed. His body fell back outta' the open door. His head was gone. Clean ripped off. We tried to close the door but it wouldn't budge. The rest of us ran. Got a mile or so back up the tunnel but it was all around us by then. Don't even know what. Like a mist we couldn't see. Thick like that. It got itself into our heads. Jimmy Duncan impaled himself on a broken piece of rail track. Didn't tell no one, just up and did it. Dave Mitchell strangled himself with his own shirt. I write this stuff down and I can't even believe it's happened. But I'm too afraid to think straight. Afraid of what, though? I ain't even seen nothin', only what being afraid has done to my friends.'"

Abby looked up at the two remaining miners across the tunnel. Their dead faces were marbleized terror. Whatever they'd seen, whatever they'd felt, was etched into their rotting flesh.

"Is there any more?" Huck asked.

"One more entry," Abby said, and continued to read.

"'May 14. I think it is, anyway. We've been in here a long time. Our first instinct was to run, and Billy Corrigan did just that, but the rest of us, the ones who are still alive, at least, we made a pact. Whatever had come outta that door, it would never leave this tunnel. We feel it, too. Right now, swirling around us. Trying to get into us. It was Bud Freewald's idea to build the wall. Took blocks from the access tunnel, pounded them together and built the strongest wall we could. It was Bud's idea for us to stay on this side of the wall. Said that whatever had gotten into us, he'd be damned if he'd let it out into the town. It's fear, is what I think. Blind, stupid fear. But I'm too afraid to think clear anymore. The lamps'll go out soon. It takes a long time to die. Even when you're prepared for it. I just wish it would be over quick. This is what you get for being strong-minded. Bud and Richard and me. We all get to watch the other ones die."

"Is that all?" Ben asked.

"That's all," Abby said.

"Now we know what happened, at least," Huck offered.

"They got scared," Abby said. "But, of what? There's nothing *real* here. It's only fear. Where did it come from? What caused the fear?"

Huck shook his head. "Did anything have to cause it?"

"What do you mean?"

"I mean, maybe fear *is* the cause," he said. "Like a storm, rolling in over the horizon. The temperature drops and your ears pop and you get a different feeling in your body. You know something's happening, but your reaction is out of proportion to the actual event."

"We're making this all up, then?" Abby asked. "The miners killed themselves because they were afraid of nothing?"

"The fear is real," Huck said. "I feel it, too. I'm feeling it right now. I'm just saying that maybe the cause of the fear isn't the real enemy."

"I don't buy it," Abby said. "There's something out there. I hope you're right, Huck, but I don't think so. There's something at the heart of all this. And I think, when we find it, we'll all have good reason to be afraid."

"I wish you hadn't said that," Ben whimpered.

"Come on, Benj, let's get this over with," Abby said. "We're in it til the end, and I think that moment is on its way."

Ben nodded and carefully set down the shovel he'd been holding. His face was pale, but he managed a tight smile.

"I'm right behind you, " he said, and they headed off into the tunnel.

Chapter Twenty-Three

Fear

The mineshaft angled sharply to the right. A few steps on, they could no longer see the miners' wall behind them. They were in uncharted territory now. Abby took hold of Ben's hand.

"Too tight," he said.

"Sorry," she replied, and released some of the pressure. It was still too tight, but Ben didn't say anything else. They walked in silence. Huck's flashlight cut strange shadows into the tunnel walls. He jerked the light this way and that, hoping to see in all directions at once.

"I wish Dad was here," Ben said.

"Me, too," Abby replied, and was surprised to realize it was the truth. There was nothing their dad could do to protect them—not even if he wanted to, which appeared to be the case. But something about his presence, his quiet Southern strength, would have gone a long way toward making things bearable.

But he wasn't there and it wasn't bearable. He was, in fact, one of the reasons they were there in the first place. It stung Abigail's already raw wounds to know her father's choice was to sacrifice her to save his wife. That wasn't the man she knew. Something wasn't sitting right. None of it made sense. Her daddy loved her. So did her mom. And it was real love, too, not the sort of knowing kindness a farmer shows to his sheep and pigs. before they're led to the slaughterhouse. Despite what she knew, despite what Gus had told her, damn it, how could it be?

"We're heading downhill," she said.

"I feel it, too," Huck agreed.

They kept walking, and the angle of the tunnel got steeper. Gravity made them walk faster, and a couple of times they nearly tripped.

"We should take a break," Ben said.

"A break?" Abby asked. "What for?"

"I gotta' pee," Ben replied. Abigail rolled her eyes.

"Well, just do it here," she said.

"I can't do it here!"

"Ben, there's no way we're going to let you go off on your own," Huck said. "Privacy isn't a luxury we have down here, I'm afraid."

Ben groaned. "All right, but at least don't shine that stupid light on me."

Huck was about to argue when Abby put a hand on his arm. They sat down together with their backs to the wall while Ben urinated a few feet away. The sound carried in the tunnel.

"How deep do these mines go?" Abby asked. Huck shrugged.

"I don't know, exactly," he said. "A few miles down, maybe more."

"It shouldn't take us too long to reach the end."

"Depending on the angle," Huck replied.

"Angle?"

"It could be several miles to walk," he said. "It's miles *down*, not just miles in."

"I don't follow."

"All right, let me show you," he said, and motioned to Abby's right. "Hand me that axe handle there, yes, that's the one. Now, if we draw a straight line this way…"

Huck used the axe handle to draw a line in the dirt of the tunnel. Instead of drawing a clear line, though, the axe handle sank two inches into the rock underneath.

"What's wrong?" Abby asked.

"It's solid granite under these hills," Huck said. "And coal embedded in that. Yet look at this."

He pushed the axe handle deeper into the rock. It made a greasy sound as it slid through.

"This rock isn't solid," he said.

"Then we'd better get moving," Abby replied. "Ben, you'd better be done 'cause we gotta' go."

Ben buttoned his pants and wiped his hands on the trouser leg. Abby thought about taking his hand again, and thought better of it. They walked side-by-side, with Huck and his flashlight trailing behind.

"This floor is funny," Ben said. "It's, like… spongy."

"You're right," Abby agreed. "It's like walking on thick grass."

"We need to keep moving," Huck said. "Quickly, now."

They did as they were told, walking faster down the incline of the tunnel until they were almost jogging.

There was a sound in the tunnel. It was almost a hissing sound, like steam escaping through a pipe. It was ahead of them, but coming their way.

"What is it?" Ben asked.

Huck shone his light down the tunnel. Its beam didn't penetrate far.

"Do we make a run for it?" Huck asked.

"Run where?" Abby replied. "Whatever it is, it's in our way."

"I think we're in *its* way," Ben countered.

"The door is down there," Abby asserted. "It's in our way."

The sound was getting closer. Its tone had changed. Instead of a hiss it had become a rip, like a piece of paper being torn in half.

"I don't like this sound," Ben said. "This is a bad sound."

"I think we'd better hold on to something," Huck suggested. "One of the wall supports, maybe. Ben's right, that sound *is* a bad sound. If it's what it sounds like…"

"What does it sound like?" Abby asked.

"You don't want to know."

Before Abby could argue, the sound changed again. It sounded like something shattering. The sound was like a dog running across a crowded dinner table, shattering everything in its path. And it was much closer than it had been before.

"Grab hold of a beam!" Huck ordered. "Quickly! And don't let go."

Abby and Ben did what they were told. They each wrapped their arms around nearby support beams lining the tunnel walls. Ben's flashlight dropped, but the rope he'd tied between it and his knapsack kept it attached. The light bounced erratically, casting insane shadows on the walls.

Beyond the glow of the bouncing flashlight, Abby saw another light appear. It moved quickly toward them, illuminating the mineshaft with a red, sinister glow.

"It's coming!" Abby yelled.

"What is it?" Ben asked.

"Who cares, it's almost here!" Huck shouted. "Hang on!"

The sound of shattering porcelain was deafening. It was all around them, echoing in the limited space. The walls and ceiling rumbled. Ben fought for his balance, and struggled to hang on.

The floor of the tunnel split down the middle. It was a rough break, like a fault line in an earthquake. Pieces of the spongy rock broke away like shattered pieces of pottery. The pieces fell into the space the fault line had opened up.

The crack in the floor widened as it passed them. Large wedges of the floor cracked and disappeared into the abyss. But it wasn't a dark nothingness, this opening in the floor. Red and blue and yellow clouds roiled like a fierce storm inside the hole. It was like standing on top of a thunderstorm, only painted in some unearthly way. Furious clouds instantly swallowed the chunks of the tunnel that fell away. The cloud layer was deep—as she looked into them, Abby wondered how far down it went.

The floor crumbled in the center, beneath the rail tracks. The metal tracks hung precariously over the shattered ledge. As the gap widened, they too were pulled down into the clouds with a stubborn whine. There was a wind now, a sucking wind that ripped at Abigail's clothing. It wasn't strong enough to pull her in—not yet, at least—but she feared it would quickly become so. She clung tighter to the support beam.

The clouds were changing. The colors were deepening and the light reflecting on the walls of the tunnel changed from red to blue. Inside the clouds, something was rising to the surface. Abby stared in horrified disbelief as faces appeared. They were hideous faces, twisted in rage and pain, contorted by sadness and misery. They cried out from inside the swirling mist.

"Help us."

"Take my hand."

"Please don't leave me here."

Waves of sadness radiated from the faces. Abby's heart sank. Tears flowed down her face. Her mother was somewhere like this, she knew it. Mom was in pain, and without hope. Abby looked at Huck, hoping his scientific detachment would ground her and steel her to the grief. But he was crying, too, overcome by the sea of pain opened at their feet. She looked at Ben.

Her brother had let go of his support beam. He knelt on the edge of the ever-widening crack, bent over like he was staring at his reflection in a river. Abby screamed.

"I can help him," Ben said, and then said to the faces in the clouds, "Take my hand, okay? I'll pull you out and then you can - -"

A hand reached out of the swirling mass. It was burned and oozed a clear liquid. Ben screamed. He tried to pull back. The hand was too quick. It grabbed his wrist.

"Ben!" Abby called.

"I can't get it off me!" Ben yelled.

Abby dropped her knapsack from her shoulder and stepped to where her brother was. She wrapped her arm around the nearest wall support and reached out for him.

"It's too strong!" Ben yelped. "It's pulling me in!"

Abby took hold of Ben's knapsack. She gave a hard tug. The pack slipped off his back.

Abby threw it to one side. His flashlight, still attached, made a thud.

"Abby, help me!" Ben hollered. Abby let go of the support beam and grabbed her brother with both hands. She pulled on his legs.

The thing that had hold of him was strong. Even one-handed, it was all Abby could do to keep hold of Ben. Her strength was giving out. She knew that in a moment she'd be too weak to hold him.

A flash of movement caught her eye. Huck was on the opposite side of the gap, against the far wall. His wild hair blew furiously in the tunnel's wind.

"Stand back, Abby," Huck said.

"I'm not letting him go!" Abby yelled.

"Trust me," Huck replied, and Abby did.

She let go of Ben's legs. He screamed, and was pulled closer to the clouds. The oozing arm had become two arms, which snaked their way up Ben's torso. He was being pulled in. In a matter of seconds, he would disappear and then she'd never - -

Huck landed with a WHAP beside Ben. The unstable edge of the hole crumbled further, and Huck had to steady himself.

"Help me!" Ben screamed.

Huck rolled over onto his stomach. He was beside Ben, close enough to nearly smother him. Huck grabbed Ben around the waist and pulled him away from the hole. The thing that had hold of him tugged harder on Ben, but Huck was stronger. Ben and Huck fell backwards against the rock wall as the arms of the creature let go.

Abby was on them in a moment, hugging Ben tightly against her.

"What are you doing?" she asked. "I almost lost you. What's wrong with you?"

"I don't know," Ben cried. "I couldn't help it. I just… I felt so helpless, watching their faces. I wanted to help them."

"It's an illusion, Ben," Huck said. "It's only make-believe."

"It sure didn't *feel* make-believe," Ben replied.

"That's because it's playing on our fears," Huck said. "It's using our emotions to take hold of us. Look, I have no doubt that what's behind all of this is real, it's just that this," he gestured at the hole in the tunnel floor, "is meant to keep us off balance."

"Then we need to fight it where it lives," Abby said. "Come on, grab hands."

They did, forming a line against the wall of the tunnel.

"It's not real," Abby said. "And it has no power if we don't let it in. Close your eyes. Imagine something that made you feel good. Something that made you feel safe. Go there, in your mind."

"I can't think of anything," Ben whined.

"Rockaway Beach," Abby said. "Remember that? When we went there with Mom and Dad?"

"We rode the streetcar," Ben replied. "It was winter time."

"There was snow on the beach," Abby said. "And we were bundled up and we made a sandy snowman."

"And the tide came in and washed it away."

"That's a good place to go, Benji," Abby said. "Remember Mom and Dad made snow angels?"

Ben smiled, his eyes tightly closed. All around them, the intensity of the destruction got louder. The ceiling was crumbling now. Abby squinted and forced herself to concentrate. She remembered the bitter cold ocean wind against their faces, and the sound of their mother's laughter as she threw a snowball at their dad. It was just them, the four of them, and there was no better place to be.

And then, as suddenly as it began, the noise around them stopped. The silence that followed was disorienting. Abigail opened her eyes.

The tunnel had returned to its original form. There was no crack in the floor, no swirling cloud of faces underneath. The rail tracks were neatly aligned. It was as if the whole thing had never happened.

"Where did it all go?" Ben asked. "The hole, the thing that grabbed me, all of it?"

"Fear is powerful," Huck said, letting go of their hands. "The world we know, our reality, is the one we perceive. We see and smell and touch the world and we filter it through our minds. Like we already talked about, Abigail, our whole existence is our own perception. Fear has an enormous power. It colors everything we see."

"But that was *real*," Ben argued. "That thing that grabbed me, I could feel it oozing over my skin."

"So where is it now?" Huck asked. "Ben, the only weapon this consciousness has is our own fear. Whatever it is that's behind all of it, I'm sure it's completely real. It's our fear that makes it strong. Nothing else."

"But I *am* afraid," Ben said. "I'm terrified."

"That's why it wins," Huck replied, and shook his head. "Fear isn't a bad thing. It's a defense mechanism that tells us to run from danger. Irrational fear, though, that's different. That's what's being used against us."

Abby sighed heavily. "It's regrouping now. I can feel it. It's angry at us, too. We're getting too close."

"Then we need to keep going," Huck said.

"Pick up your packs and let's go," Abby ordered. She slipped her own over her shoulders and started walking.

The tunnel narrowed. The walls got closer together. Not much, and not quickly, but it was evident. The rail tracks wound off into another shaft. Abby knew they were close to the end of the tunnel.

Close to the door.

Ben and Huck shone their lights ahead of them. Their weakening beams didn't penetrate far into the gloom. Before long, they'd go out. Abby hoped they'd reach the end before that happened.

"What was that?" Ben asked. He spun around, flashing his light behind him.

"What was what?" Abby replied.

"There was a sound back there," Ben said. "A scuttling sound, like an animal."

"Relax, Benji," Abby told him.

"Stop calling me Benji!"

"I'll call you whatever I want to call you."

"Knock it off."

"Benji."

"Freckle-head."

"Hey, stop that," Huck was exasperated. "There's nothing back there except what our minds dream up, and acting like spoiled little brats isn't going to - -"

Before he could finish, something knocked him off his feet. His flashlight landed a foot away, rolling backwards onto the rail tracks. Abby looked into the gloom behind them.

Two red eyes glowed in the darkness. A low growl echoed down the tunnel. Whatever it was kept to the shadows. Huck crawled toward his flashlight.

"I don't care what you think you see," Huck said. "There's nothing - - AAUGH!"

The thing that wasn't there took hold of Huck's legs. It pulled him off the ground and raised him up until he was hanging upside down near the top of the tunnel.

Ben dropped his light. It landed at his feet and rolled away. It stopped when the rope attached to his pack had played out.

"Shine your light on it!" Huck cried. "It's not real. Shine your light on it!"

"I dropped it!" Ben yelled.

"Pick it up!" Huck cried.

"Wait, I think I can..."

"Ben, it's attached to the string!" Abby said. "On your pack. Just pull on the string."

Ben did as she instructed, and the flashlight reversed course back to his hand.

Huck was thrashed like a rag doll. He cried out in pain as his shoulder hit the wall.

Ben pulled the flashlight off the ground. He aimed it at Huck. For a moment, a brief instant, he saw the thing that held Browntree. It was huge and lumbering, with a tusk-covered face and black fur that rippled in the light. And then it was gone, and Huck fell heavily to the floor. He cried out as something snapped.

"Huck!" Abby yelled, and was at his side in a moment.

"I broke my damned leg," he said, more angry than pained.

"Are you sure?" Abby asked.

"Of course I'm sure," Huck snapped. "Didn't you hear it crack?"

"Can you walk?" Ben asked.

"With some help," Huck said. He sighed. "I don't supposed either of you have ever made a tourniquet?"

"I don't even know what that is," Ben replied.

"No, I thought not," Huck groaned. "I'll walk you through it. I'll slow you down, but there's no way I'm staying here alone."

"We're almost at the end, anyway," Abby said. "We should be at the door soon."

"Good," Huck replied. "I've had about all I can take on this little expedition."

Ben and Abby followed Huck's terse instructions, and tried the best they could to immobilize his broken leg.

Chapter Twenty-Four

The Door

The tourniquet they rigged up was crude; a couple of splintered pieces of wall beams lashed together with rope, but it was good enough to keep him mobile. Huck hobbled between them. Ben and Abby helped him keep his weight off his broken leg. They moved slowly.

"I feel like a fool," Huck said.

"What for?" Abby asked.

"I let it get the better of me," he replied. "I knew it wasn't real and yet I bought into it, hook, line and sinker."

"It was real enough," Ben said, and shuddered.

"We're almost there," Abby told them. In another few steps, Ben's dim flashlight beam showed them their search had ended.

The door was as Billy Corrigan had described it. It was as tall as the tunnel, ten feet high. Wide bands of rusted metal crisscrossed the door. Enormous metal rivets held everything in place. It looked like it belonged on a castle. It was utterly out of place at the end of a mineshaft.

"What do we do now?" Ben asked.

"I don't know," Abby replied. "Knock?"

"I don't think it's locked," Huck said.

"No, I don't think so, either," Abby agreed. They stood in front of it as Ben's flashlight got dimmer and dimmer.

"What are we waiting for?" Huck asked.

"My nerve," Abby replied.

"You have a job to do," Huck said softly. "I would take it away from you if I could. I'd give near about anything if we could turn around right now and leave this place. But we can't."

"I know."

"You're the one who has to do this," Huck whispered.

Abigail reached out and took hold of the handle. It was round, neatly polished and carved with a strange symbol. Abby paused, her hand on the large round door handle.

"I've seen this before," Abby said.

"Mom's necklace," Ben nodded.

"Our mother had a necklace with this same symbol," Abigail explained. "I remember she wore it a lot right before she died. I'd never seen it before. She'd never worn it."

"It's a Celtic knot," Huck said. "But I've never seen one so intricate. That's a dragon's head, and a lion. The carving's remarkable."

"She's here, isn't she?" Ben asked. Abby nodded.

"I think so."

Abigail turned the handle. It moved easily, and they heard a resounding CLICK inside the door. Abby pulled the massive door. It didn't move.

"It is locked," she said.

Huck grinned. "Try pushing it."

She did, and the door opened easily. So easily, in fact, that it seemed to be doing so of its own volition. Abby let go of the handle. The heavy door continued to swing open.

On the other side was darkness. Ben shone his flashlight inside, but it was too weak to penetrate. In another moment, the light went dead completely. They stood in total blackness. Somewhere far off, water was dripping.

"Stay together," Abigail said.

"Where else are we going to go?" Ben replied, and they stepped through the door.

A wooden floor creaked under their feet. Abby smelled wood smoke and something else, too. It was a bitter smell, like fruit that had gone over.

A match was struck and by its light Abby watched as a fire was lit. Warmth and light took hold and she realized where she was.

"Why are we here?" she asked.

The Red Witch stood up from the fire and wiped soot from her skirt. By the firelight, Abby saw she was inside the Witch's cabin. The furniture was all there, the two chairs, the stone mantelpiece, the woven rug in front of the fire. Beyond their small sphere, though, there was only blackness. Abigail had a sense of vast distances beyond it, as if they were standing in the middle of a cavernous black nothing.

"What were you expecting?" the Witch asked.

"Is this what the miners saw?" Abby asked. "Are you what scared them to death?"

"This is what you see," the Red Witch replied. "Everyone is different."

Abby realized then that Ben and Huck weren't with her. She spun around, reaching out blindly for them.

"Your reality, not theirs," the Witch said.

"Bring them back."

"Not my job."

"Where did they - -?"

"You spend so much time worrying about where," the Witch shook her head. "Where am I? Where's my mommy? *Where* is of no consequence."

"My mother."

"Is alive, yes, of course she is. But why you would still want to find her after learning the truth… she had you in order to destroy you. For her own gain. She was tired, just like we all are. The mortal world is tiresome. Wars and floods and pestilence and love. The worst one of all, that love business. They keep getting hurt and they keep coming back for more. At least with the floods, it wipes them out. Love just hollows them."

"You prefer fear?"

"Now *that's* an emotion I can sink my teeth into," the Witch said. "Terror has such a lovely aftertaste."

"It was you, then?" Abby asked. "The town, the things in the woods, the Goners?"

"Of course not," the Witch replied. "Mine is an immortal existence, but my limits are strict. I feed only on the residue. Like your mother. I don't create it."

"Then what does?"

"Who knows? I've never seen it. There are glimpses of it, certainly, but to set eyes on it is to pass into a realm I am not able to penetrate. It is Beyond."

"Beyond?"

"Past the world of life and death, there is a place called Beyond. Living and dying is easy. Beyond, well… it's beyond."

"Is that where my mother is?"

The Red Witch shook her head. "Why are you still fixating on her? She's gone. You can't find her."

"Is that where she is?"

"*Where* again."

"Is that where she - -?"

"Yes, that's where I sent her," the Witch said. "Forever bound to the Beyond. You can't reach her. No one can. Let her go. You have more important work to do."

"Such as?"

"Such as, letting me die!" the Witch roared. The fire flared and a fury of sparks burst onto the wood floor.

"I'm not afraid of you," Abigail said.

"I know."

"Then how do you expect to - -?"

The Witch raised one obese arm and a circle of light appeared above her. Abigail gasped. Ben was there, and he was afraid.

"Abby!" he called. "Abby, help me!"

"Ben!"

"You don't fear me, but you fear for him," the Witch said. "That is my weapon."

"Let him go!"

"Give me what I need."

"No!"

Ben was drowning. Thick, black ooze seeped over his chest. He sputtered and spat it out of his mouth.

"Give me what I need, child, and your mortal brother lives another day."

Abby felt a dark fury rise in her belly. She'd never felt such hatred. It sickened her, the feeling did. She had no control over it. It was a fire that raged and grew with each breath she took. The wooden floorboards trembled. Abigail's legs felt weak. The fury that grew in her overwhelmed her body. It was a foreign thing, not part of her but traveling through her like a electrical current. Every hair on her body, arms and neck and head, stood on end. She was alive with the energy. Every cell felt supercharged.

"Let my brother go," Abigail said.

"Give me what I need," the Witch replied, but she was afraid. The energy inside Abigail was palpable. The Witch backed away.

Abby felt the energy burst like a tidal surge. It was the same feeling she'd had the first time she'd been in the Witch's cabin, but this time it was much more intense. A sonic boom of energy expelled from her body. It flattened everything in its path, chairs, fireplace, the fire itself. The Red Witch rolled head over heels into the darkness. The cabin was gone, the light was gone, and Abby was in blackness again. Slowly, deliberately, the world brightened. The blackness around her cracked, breaking apart like an eggshell. Light so white it threatened to blind her enveloped the room. There was no heat, but the light's intensity made her curl up into a ball on the ground.

She stayed like that for a long time. She listened to the world break apart around her. Abby heard voices. There were hundreds of them, but above their din she heard one most distinctly.

"Open your eyes, Abigail."

Abby did. White light blinded her, but she shielded her eyes.

"Mom?"

"I'm here."

Abigail struggled to look up. The light was too bright, and she had to keep her eyes covered.

"I can't see you."

"You know I'm here."

"Yes."

"That will have to do for now."

Tears fell from Abby's eyes.

"Where are you?" she asked.

"Beyond," her mother replied. "But safe. For now."

"I have to find you."

"I don't think even you can do that," her mother said. "But you need to hear what I'm going to tell you."

"Mom, I miss you."

"And I miss you."

"They've told me things," Abby said. "Horrible things, Mom. About you."

"I know."

"Tell me they're not true."

"Were that they weren't," her mother said. "I wish I could tell you that everything you've heard was lies."

"No."

"It's all true," her mother said. "I am a Walker, and I came to Sunset Falls in order to find a way to die. The only way was to produce a girl child with a mortal man and then use the child, use you, to cross over."

"Mom, no!"

"But the part you didn't hear, not from the Red Witch, nor from anyone else, is that I had a change of heart. After I felt you growing inside me, and after I began to feel love for you, I couldn't do it. I told your father and together we left Sunset Falls. He didn't judge me for what I had intended to do, only how I righted that wrong. I didn't know in what terrible a state I'd left things. Your Uncle Dutch and his foolish jealousy… that's what the Witch used to find me. She banished me to the Beyond knowing that your father would try to find me, and that you would be sent to the only family you had left. Dutch hated your father's happiness and fabricated his love for me in order to hate Galen even more. We're all tied together, aren't we, no matter how far away we run? It was Dutch who sent me to the Beyond. Not out of love, but out of spite for his brother."

"Mom, I don't care about any of it," Abby said. "I love you, and none of the rest of it matters."

"Oh, Abigail, you have no idea how long I've waited to hear you say that."

"Mom, tell me where you are," Abby implored. "Tell me how to get there. I'll come for you, no matter what I have to do."

"You can't come for me, my darling. You need to move on. You and your brother and your dad, let me go."

"Mom, no!" Abby shrieked. "I'll find you, I promise I will, Mom, I promise, I'll - -"

She opened her eyes. She was in the forest, in a clearing. The rumble of Sunset Falls was nearby.

"She's awake!" Ben said. Abby pushed his hot hands away from her.

"Get off me, Ben, we've got to find… Ben?" she yelped, and hugged him tight.

"Thank God," Huck said.

"We thought you were…" Ben began, but choked on the last word.

"Not yet," Abby replied.

"But what happened?" Ben asked.

"I think it's over," Abby said. "This part of it, anyway."

"The Witch?" Huck asked. Abby shook her head.

"I don't think she's still here."

"Is she dead?" Ben asked.

"No," Abby replied. "But gone. I think she's done with this place."

Chapter Twenty-Five

The Wild Card

"We were here the whole time," Ben said. "We stepped through the door after you and we ended up here."

"You were unconscious," Huck added. "And not breathing."

"We thought you were dead," Ben said.

Abby explained what she'd seen, from her battle with the Red Witch to her conversation with their mother. Ben wiped his eyes.

"What do we do now?" he asked.

"Find a doctor to set Huck's leg," Abby said. "Then who knows? Find Dad, probably."

"So it's not over yet?" Ben asked.

"Not for me," Abby replied.

They hoisted Huck up to stand and started walking in the direction of town. The woods were calm. Sunset Falls was peaceful again.

"I wonder if this part's really over," Huck said. "Whatever destroyed the town, I mean."

"Not over," Abby replied. "Just beaten."

"Like the Witch," Ben said.

Aunt Penny stepped out of the woods. She wore an apron, and a green print dress Abby had seen her wear many times before.

"You made it, then?" she asked.

"We did," Abby replied.

Penny pursed her lips, as if tasting something sour.

"I want you to know I bear no ill will," she said. "I was a fool myself to listen to Dutch. A weak man. A slave to his vices."

"Where is he? We left him in Dr. Browntree's cabin."

"No one knows," Penny said. "Ran off, most likely. Dalton Freewald found him there, set him loose. He took off. No one's seen hide nor hair of him. For the best, though. That sounds like an awful thing t'say, don't it?"

Abby lowered her eyes.

"I ain't extended any sort of kindness to you since you been here," Penny said. "Either of you. An' that ain't like me. It ain't how I was raised. We're kin, after all. Even if it's just by marriage, it don't make it any weaker than if it was blood. I apologize for how I been actin' t'ward ya'. An' I wanna' bury the hatchet. C'mon, let's you an' me give us a hug an' start up fresh."

"I'd like that," Abigail said. Ben took Huck's weight and Abby walked the few steps toward her Aunt Penny. She reached out her arms to embrace the older woman.

The knife was hidden in the pocket of Penny's apron. She drew it with expert precision. She'd planned it—the whole thing was perfectly timed. How long and with how much malice of forethought, only she knew. Abigail couldn't react. Her forward motion impaled her against the blade, and Penny's thick hands drove it home deep into her breast.

For a moment, it looked like they were embracing. Abby's hands went up to catch her fall, and clamped hard onto Penny's bony shoulders. Penny's left arm, the one not holding the knife, wrapped around Abby's waist to draw the girl closer.

Ben screamed first. He dropped Huck, who fell heavily to the ground. Abigail turned her head to the sound of Ben's scream. She shouted at him to stay back. Except no sound came out, only a sputtering of blood that stained her lips.

Penny withdrew the knife. Abby pulled away from her. Her entire body ached, not just where she was stabbed. Abby stumbled backwards. Penny lifted the knife above her head, intending to lunge forward.

A single gunshot pierced the still woods. A spray of blood exited Penny's temple. The old woman fell to the ground. It took Abby a long moment to realize what had happened. She looked up the trail.

The man who came running had a familiar confident gait and long strides.

"Dad?" Ben said.

Galen Crosley caught his daughter as she fell. Blood spurted from her chest. Her mouth was full of the stuff. She wanted to spit it out, but every move she made hurt too much.

"Oh, God, Abby!" her father said. He laid her down on the path. Ben fell to his knees at her side.

"Daddy?" Abby called. She coughed, and blood spattered the front of her father's shirt.

Ben stripped off his own shirt and watched as his father packed it over Abby's wound. It was soaked through almost instantly.

"Damn," Galen hissed. "Abby, stay awake. Stay with me."

Abigail floated in and out of consciousness. Her vision got blurry, then blackened all together.

"I see it," she said. The clarity of her voice made both Galen and Ben stop.

"You see what, honey?" Galen asked.

"The Beyond," Abby said. "They're taking me now. You can find me. You can get there. It can be done."

"Find you?" Galen asked. "What are ya - - ?"

"I'll find you, Abby," Ben said. "I know what to do."

"I love you, Benji," she whispered.

Ben smiled. Tears blurred his vision.

"Don't call me Benji."

"I'll call you anything I…"

Then she was gone. Her head lolled to one side. The bleeding from her chest subsided. Galen threw back his head and screamed. It was a combination of fury and pain, and everyone in the town of Sunset Falls felt it like their own.

Ben knelt over his sister's silent face and wiped the fiery red hair out of her eyes. He put his hand over her eyes, closing them for a final time.

"I'll find you, Abby," Ben said, and began to sob.

"'When sunset falls in Sunset Falls'," Ben said.

"What's that?" Huck asked.

Ben shook his head. "A stupid poem Aunt Penny told us when we first came. Meant to scare us, I think."

"Did it?"

Ben laughed. "You bet it did."

"Are you scared now?" Huck asked.

Ben thought about this.

"Not scared," he said. "Scared is for little kids. I'm afraid now."

"What's the difference?"

Ben smiled. "Scared paralyzes you. Afraid, well, you can still get the job done."

"Afraid is good," Galen added. "Especially now."

"Just as long as it's fear of something real," Huck said. "Imagined fear will just shut you down."

"I think we're ready," Ben said.

"I don't think we'll ever be ready," his dad said, and grinned. "You're in charge on this one, Ben. I ain't sure what you got in mind, but you seem pretty goldarned confident about it."

"I am," Ben replied.

"So where will you start?" Huck asked.

Ben sat on the windowsill of Huck's hospital room. He was no longer the terrified little boy who had followed his sister off the bus into Sunset Falls. There was a ruggedness about him now, a shadow of the man he was on his way to becoming. He glanced out the window as the first snow of the season fell over Charleston, West Virginia.

"You'll be okay here?" Ben asked.

"Until the pain medicine runs out," Huck replied. "And you didn't answer my question."

Ben grinned. "Nope."

Huck shook his head, but didn't push for any more. He'd learned enough about the Crosleys to know that he'd have more luck spinning straw into gold than changing their minds once they'd gotten them set on something.

"Be careful," was all he could say.

"We will," Ben replied. He went to Huck's bedside and gave his friend a hug. Huckleberry Browntree was his friend now. Events had made it so. They'd proven themselves to each other. That was the nature of friendship, and of love.

Ben pulled his knapsack over his shoulder. It was a new one... new to him, anyway. It was Army surplus from the Great War, and it was far too big for him. It carried everything he needed, though, and that was what mattered.

"We're going to find my family now," Ben said.

"I'm anxious to meet your mother," Huck replied.

Galen shook Huck's hand and followed his son out the door. Huck listened to the sound of their boots echoing down the hallway. He wondered if he'd ever see them again. He couldn't tell. Speculation wasn't his specialty. He dealt in hard facts. He was a man of science, after all.

Printed in the United States
143037LV00003BA/5/P